ENCOUNTER

ENCOUNTER

J. HUNTER HOLLY

WILDSIDE PRESS

ENCOUNTER

Published in 2007 by Wildside Press.
www.wildsidepress.com

PART ONE

He crashed. The ship plummeted into the Arkansas hills, a glowing, shining, silent thing. There was no fire when it hit ground, only the loud thud of impact and the sudden rending of trees. He felt the first jolt, then nothing more.

CHAPTER ONE

Li moved about the cabin, getting supper. Over the sizzle of food she heard Josha whistling out in the woods, and the dog barked at some runaway rabbit.

In the dim light her hair stood out wildly from her head, making a tangled halo of wisps, but the wrinkles on her face were smoothed over and her dress didn't look quite so faded. Haphazardly she set tin plates on the table and got down the cups. By that time the smell had brought the dog yipping through the yard, and Li went to wait for Josha.

He came out of the woods fifty yards up, a bird dangling from his hand, the gun over his other shoulder. Tall and skinny, he walked with long strides, his knees ready to push through faded spots on his pants. "Evenin' Li," he called, looking up from the ground.

She answered with his name "Josha," making it both a greeting and an affection. When he was a few yards off, she went in to finish the supper and he followed, hanging the bird in the corner, high up so the dog couldn't reach it. Then he sat down and held up his fork, waiting. She dished up their stew and set down a plate for the dog.

"You shouldn't go given' thet to the dog, Li," Josha scolded.

"Jist a little won't hurt none," she answered.

She sat down across from the man and started to eat.

They spent every evening in the chairs outside the cabin, sharing something together. Li couldn't name what it was they shared. It was just being quiet together.

Josha was in the big chair, cleaning the gun; and she sat with her hands pressed in her lap, watching chickens disappear to roost and the dog poke around in the brush. She was looking to the north when she suddenly straightened and whispered, "Josha!"

He followed her gaze upward. He saw it too.

"What is it, Josha?" she asked with a trembling voice.

He didn't know. It was wider than it was thick and it was all purple glow. It didn't make a sound but streaked in toward them fast. It flashed over, growing lower until they saw it break the tops off trees and fall into the taller ones, pushing through to hit against the rise of the next hill. It made a strange noise when it hit and they could see it glowing down inside the trees for a while. It grew dim and went out.

They watched in frightened silence, then turned to each other. "Never seen nothin' like thet afore," Josha said.

"No," Li answered.

"S'pose it was one of them meteors?" he asked.

"They don't never come down, Josha. They jist fly out there, back and forth. They never come to ground."

They looked again at the place where it had fallen and moved in accord to go into the cabin. Li turned up the lamps and sat down in the rocker to stare at the flames on the hearth. Then quickly she brightened. "I don't think it's nothin' to be scared of. The dog ain't been howlin', and he's sure to howl if it's anythin' unnatural."

"Thet's right, Li. The dog'd sure howl." He sat back but raised up again. "Where'd he go?"

"I ain't seen him around since afore the thing come down. He was pokin' in the brush, last I know."

It was a long time before the noise came, shrill and nasal outside the door. They stood up together, trembling. It was the dog, but he had never made such a sound before. His mangy tail was sticking up under his legs, the tip wagging weakly against his thin stomach.

Josha knelt and took the dog's head in his big hands. He rubbed him with long, hard strokes from head to tail, rubbing away the stiffness the way he rubbed cramps from his own muscles.

Soon the dog responded and relaxed, but with the loosening he trembled until he had to crouch. He pushed his ears back, eyes half shut, and faced the door, growling low.

*****

Ed Moor taxied his red Piper up the runway and stopped. He was numb. The fear had fled, leaving cold emptiness behind. But there was something else he hadn't expected — an eerie feeling, a "spook" as his wife, Grace, said.

He thought a lot on the drive home and decided if Al Simpson still wanted to buy the Piper, he wouldn't quibble any longer. But it was ridiculous that he should sell just because he had seen something that scared him. "Stupid," he said aloud to himself.

He thought maybe it was like being in the presence of God, only it wouldn't be God. That thing radiated evil. Yes, that was better. Radiated evil that some tiny part of your brain recognized, and functioning for the first time, told you to run.

As he walked through the kitchen door, he caught the scent of freshly brewed coffee and knew he'd only need to call, "I'm home," and she'd be there, sharing coffee and chatter.

But he didn't call right away. He wanted time to think — alone. But Grace heard him come in and snapped off the television set in the middle of a detective story. She was the only person he'd ever known who could do that.

"What happened, Ed!" she exclaimed, seeing her husband. "You look like you've had a scare."

"I did. A big one. It's a funny thing, Grace. And it's hard to believe."

"Do you want to tell me?"

"You're the only one I can tell." He had been flying out over the hills, he said, when he caught sight of something out of the corner of his eye.

"It was coming out of the northwest — fast. It came right at me, starting out small and getting bigger and lower all the time." He wiped his forehead. "It was the darndest thing, Grace. Big, sort of wheel-like, and it was glowing; that's the only word for it — glowing. It was white and purple together, and there wasn't any sound, and there wasn't anything behind it — no trail or anything. It was like I was standing still in a vacuum and this big thing was going by.

"I went after it the best I could. I couldn't catch it. It got lower until it started tearing up the trees, and then it sank down. I could see it glowing in the woods. Before I got close enough to really see anything, it had died out — just like that. It faded and glowed weaker and then it just died."

He came to the hardest part. "I was scared and I got out of there. It wasn't so bad seeing it — it was the 'feeling' I got off of it. I can't explain. It's the kind of thing that makes a dog howl. It was worse right over the spot; it sort of came up strong there. Anyway, I got out of there and came on home."

Grace's forehead furrowed. "Don't you think you'd better report it to someone who can investigate?"

"Not on your life!" His voice was loud and emphatic. "I'm not reporting this to anybody. We'll keep this to ourselves. I don't want anything more to do with it. I'm going to tell Al he can buy my plane." He didn't like the belligerent tone in his voice, but it pushed out in spite of him. "I'm through with flying."

CHAPTER TWO

Morning came creeping through the trees and poked into the cabin where Li and Josha waited. They had not stirred and they had not slept, but with morning the fearful shadows disappeared and Josha unbarred the door.

The dog jumped to his feet, habit forcing him toward his usual dash for the outside where small things were just beginning to stir. But he stopped silent on the sill, head up, sniffing the air. He didn't budge one step farther.

Li's eyes met her husband's, questioning; and he mumbled, "Ain't nothin' out there. Least as far as I kin see."

"Suppose I should git some food on?" she said.

Josha stayed near the window, his eyes roaming the clearing around the cabin. The chickens were scavenging, unaware of every-thing except their beaks pecking in the dirt. Farther up the hill to the right, a curl of smoke told him their son Luke and Min, his wife, were up. He had never minded their being so far away before.

Li called him to the table and they ate silently. Then she looked up, her face alarmed by a new thought. "Josha, supposin' what we saw last night was one of them big airplanes thet crashed."

"It weren't no airplane. It didn't make no noise."

"But maybe the motors were busted."

He rubbed his chin. "So, what if it was an airplane?"

"Maybe there was people in it thet was hurt. They could be lyin' there yit, fer all we know."

He wanted to say no, but years of honesty forced him to nod in assent.

"Well!" she sighed in relief. "If thet's what it was, then there's no call to be so scary, is there?"

"Except thet we'll have to go over and find out now."

The relief left her face and her mouth pulled tight at the corners as fear crept back. "If it was an airplane, then probably all the people are dead anyways."

Josha stood up, his expression tense and a bit angry. "We can't take thet chance. Can't let people die jist cause we're scared of somethin' we seen. You comin' with me?"

*****

The grass was still damp underfoot as they made their way through the woods. A strange silence hung in the air, disturbed only by the occasional *brawkk* of the chickens. Bees zoomed by, hunting for flowers, and wasps buzzed in the damp places, but even with these sounds, the stillness was oppressive.

They came upon it quickly, with no warning. Trees stood broken with shredded leaves and rents in the bark where the thing had struck them in passing. A bit farther up, saplings were bent double and large limbs hung to the ground.

Josha halted, waiting for Li to catch up. There was no sign of the brown that would mean scorching. But there had been no fire. He motioned to Li to keep close and walked slowly into the center of the turbulence of the night before.

When he saw it, he didn't realize what it was. It was partially buried in the earth when it had made contact; the rest of it loomed high to the tops of the lesser trees.

Josha grabbed Li and they huddled together, eyes riveted on the rounded thing pointing to the sky. It was like a huge, solid wheel, on end stuck in the ground.

"It ain't no airplane," Josha murmured.

"No," Li answered softly, "but it's a machine, jist the same. A machine fer men. See them windows?"

Far up on the grey machine, there were three round holes, covered over with a sort of shininess that had to be glass. None of them was broken.

"Windows," Josha said. "Thet means thet there must be men in it. There was nothin' to be scared of at all. We jist listened to a foolish old dog thet didn't know nothin'."

Li pulled away, stepping high over fallen branches. "Where you goin'?" he called.

"To look fer the men. They must be hurt here somewheres."

Josha started off in the opposite direction, eyes open for signs, pondering the strange shape of the machine. It could only be something new, some kind of plane he hadn't heard about. He spotted an open place that looked like a door and edged up until he could see inside.

The door was tipped nearly sideways from the list of the ship and he had to cock his head to get the right perspective. The place was empty. It was small, with only one chair. There were rows of knobs and dials around the walls, but they held no interest for him.

The one chair, Josha figured, meant one man; and he wasn't inside so he must have gotten out through the door. Josha looked at the ground; there was a faint track as though something had been dragged across the grass, and one or two brownish spots.

He called to Li and followed the trail. Li's foot overturned a leaf and revealed a bright piece of metal, small and button-like. It had a figure of some kind on it, and printing. They tried to make it out, but the figure was unknown to them and neither of them could read.

The trail was easier to follow then, for it was smeared with stains. It led into a bed of ferns; and as Josha pushed back the first leaves, he saw the toe of a boot. Li clawed at the bent stalks, holding them out of the way with her elbows. A man was lying there, motionless and twisted. Josha grabbed his feet and dragged him out of the cover.

"Oh," Li cried, covering her mouth. "He's hurt bad."

The man lay at their feet, his left pant leg torn and caked with blood, one arm still seeping from a cut near the wrist. Josha turned him over to rest on his back. His face was streaked with dirt and red with scratches.

"He musta' crawled in there fer protection," Josha muttered. "Probably thought some animal would git him."

"He's not very old," Li clucked, kneeling to push black hair from the man's forehead. "A handsome poor thing. We shoulda come last night, Josha."

"Well, we didn't. Now let's get him back home."

Transporting the prone man presented a problem. They tried to revive him; but there wasn't a flicker of life, except a weak, erratic pulse. Josha didn't want to carry him; the way was too long.

"Start weavin' them ferns and some of them light branches into a mat. I'll get some poles and we'll drag him back."

When the mat was finished and the poles assembled, Josha took his cord belt and some proffered strips of Li's petticoat and lashed them all together into a rude travois. Then he dragged the man onto it and tied Li's shawl under his arms and around the whole contraption.

"I think he'll stay on all right," he said, "but you better keep beside him and see he don't slip."

The travois worked well, considering the way it had been thrown together. And in spite of the load, the way home seemed shorter to Josha than the way coming. He had a man behind him — something he could understand.

As they came into their clearing, a black, shiny nose poked through the cabin door and the dog appeared, trembling on the sill. He sniffed the air, raised a quivering foot, then leaped away with a full bay, disappearing into the brush.

Josha grunted and dragged the travois into the cabin. He laid it down beside the one bed and with Li's help transferred the man from the fern mat to the lumpy mattress. He stood back and wiped his beard. "I guess the next part's up to you, Li."

Time went quickly as Li worked over the unconscious man. As she rinsed the dirt from his face and uncovered strong, broad features, she grew excited. There was a slight resemblance there to Lem, her other son, who had died.

In a while, she had him clean, bandaged, and warm under a pile of quilts. She came outside where Josha was sitting, watching for the dog, and plumped herself down in her chair.

"I kin only set a minute," she sighed happily. "I gotta boil up some broth fer him."

"Will he be all right, do you think?" Josha asked.

"In time," she answered importantly. "He appeared to be a strong man. It'd take more'n the trouble he's got to kill him."

"I suppose I should start fer The Corners and report what we found," Josha suggested halfheartedly.

"Not yit. Let him git well first. There's plenty of time fer talkin' about it later."

"And you'd like to keep him around fer a spell."

"Sure, I would. I ain't scared to admit it. A woman's used to takin' care of menfolks, and I ain't had none but you since Luke went off and married Min." She looked down at her wrinkled hands lying on the gingham dress and blushed. "It makes me feel sort of young agin, you know?" She raised her eyes shyly to her husband. "Josha, I' d — like to tell you somethin'."

"Well, what is it, woman?" Josha urged.

"It's a name fer him."

"A name? Likely he's got his own name."

"I know thet," Li pouted. "But he's asleep; and he can't tell us his own name, so I thought we should have somethin' to call him by 'stead of 'thet man,' so to speak."

Josha sighed deeply. "What name did you think of?"

"You know how he come? In thet big glowing machine? Well, I figure it sort of looked like a wheel comin' thet way — like in the Bible the preacher read us. I always remembered thet story about the wheel and tried to imagine it. Now I seen it and I want to call him fer it. I want to call him Ezekiel. It's fittin'."

CHAPTER THREE

It took a week for the dog to make up his mind to come home, and then he wouldn't cross the clearing. He stayed deep in the brush, poked his nose through the leaves, and whimpered. Josha and Li made two trips out to him every day, taking him bits of food.

The man Li called Ezekiel continued to lie motionless under the quilts. The wounds seared over and the scratches disappeared, but there was no flicker of life from him. Li stayed near by, washing, feeding, bandaging.

At noon on the tenth day, Li rushed out of the cabin. "Josha! Josha — he's goin' to wake up. Hurry!"

Josha came at a run from the woodpile; and his eyes caught the stirring of life Li had seen. Ezekiel was clutching the quilts, hands tight; and his head rocked back and forth on the pillow. His mouth opened once or twice, spasmodically; and then with no warning, his eyes flashed open.

Li grasped Josha's arm. The eyes were unaccountably dark, the nearest thing to black she had ever seen; and they were large. They stared at her in alert challenge. There was no puzzlement, no question in them; just challenge and appraisal. Li was pleased with the eyes.

"You're awake, Ezekiel," she smiled. "You're finally awake. How do you feel, boy?"

Ezekiel made no answer. Josha mumbled. "Maybe he's scared. After all he don't know where he's at."

"Of course, you don't," Li said to the man. "Well, this here's Josha and I'm Li. We found you and brung you home with us."

"Do you suppose he's deaf, Josha?" Li spurted. "Suppose he can't hear us?"

"No, he knows when you talk."

"Then what could it be?"

"I was thinkin', maybe he don't speak English."

Li smiled indulgently. "Thet's a foolish notion now. He's jist like you and me."

"Thet don't matter. There are lots of foreigners. Maybe he's one of them."

*****

Ezekiel's silence continued for days. Although he couldn't answer, Li pestered him with questions and kept up a steady monologue as she worked about the cabin. She kept the chickens out as best she could, but it took a constant battle. Then one morning even the old hen who was accustomed to laying her eggs in the sewing basket stayed outside. Li didn't stop to wonder why. It was the season for the first flies and they were bother enough. But just when they were becoming a nuisance, they, too, disappeared.

In the evenings Li sat with Josha in front of the cabin, but now there was something to talk about where there hadn't been before. Josha listened patiently. He was glad to see Li happy, but the evening was a time for quiet and he wished things hadn't changed so much.

Then came the night when Li was saying, "Ezekiel's doin' fine, Josha. He's a beautiful boy — sort of like Lem, you know? About the same age, too, I figure. Thirty-five or thereabouts."

Josha answered gently, "He ain't Lem, though; and I don't want you to git too set on him. He'll be leavin'."

Li's face twisted for only a moment, then relaxed again. "Thet's in the future. Maybe if he never talks, he won't be able to —" She broke off, her attention caught by a strange sight at the edge of the clearing.

It was the dog, half crawling, half walking toward them, his legs wobbly, reluctant to continue, yet raised each time by the will to come. Gradually he walked more surely, losing the cringe until he was trotting forward. Josha reached out a hand; but the dog went around it, straight into the cabin.

Li caught Josha's arm as he started to rise. "Let him go. He's makin' his peace finally."

*****

The next two days Ezekiel remained under the covers, gathering strength and color, eating the stews Li cooked for him and watching the dog romp about the cabin. Josha was contented and pushed his prickling thoughts away whenever they came. It was the dog. Whenever Ezekiel was petting him, the creature would have nothing to do with anyone else.

Then Josha forgot about the dog in worry over Li. When he came home from the woods one evening, she met him at the door, her forehead wrinkled with pain and her hand pressing her head. After he had rubbed her temples for a time, the pain slackened; but it never left her entirely. Josha stayed close, helping her, trying to make her rest; but she wouldn't let him near Ezekiel. On the second day he was ready to go up the hill for Min when something happened that obscured everything else. Ezekiel spoke.

It was noon and Li had carried his dish to him. He took it in his hands, cast his black eyes on her and murmured, "I thank you, Li."

She whirled to her husband, then back to the stranger. "Did you really say somethin'?" she cried. "Did you really speak?"

"I thank you," Ezekiel answered. The words came slowly from his mouth, one at a time as though they were new to him.

Immediately, Li bombarded him with questions, urging him to answer; but not another word came from him.

"Let him eat now, Li," Josha said. "Give him his time."

"You're right," she said, putting a spoon in Ezekiel's bowl. "But didn't I tell you so? He kin speak. He is jist like us."

The rest of the day passed in waiting for another word to find Ezekiel's tongue. But there was no other word. At supper time, he repeated, "I thank you," and that was all.

While she was thinking about Ezekiel, Li could almost forget the headache that had been steadily plaguing her; the rest of the time it throbbed on, harder and stronger. When she was seated before the cabin at night, she couldn't even watch the stars.

*****

The next day Josha got up with the sun, said his usual unanswered good morning to Ezekiel and ate quickly. Then he started out for Min's. Luke was his only living son and they didn't visit back and forth often, but enough.

He had reached the white rock that marked the halfway point to Luke's when something made him stop.

One hundred yards farther up, he stopped again. He didn't understand it, but something told him to go home. His feet almost had a will of their own, wanting to go back.

Josha turned around and headed down the hill, the smoke from his cabin drawing him like a beacon. He hurried through the trees, oblivious to everything except the smoke and the way.

Li appeared at the door, her face happy. "Josha, how did you git back so soon?"

"I didn't go." He scratched his head.

"There's no need any more," she said. "The pain's all gone. It left sudden, like it never was there at all."

He met her eyes, confused, but the look of relief and joy in them made everything all right.

She pulled on his sleeve. "I've got another surprise fer you."

He followed her into the cabin, glancing automatically at Ezekiel's bed. But Ezekiel wasn't there. Li laughed behind him and he swiveled to meet Ezekiel head on, eye to eye. The man stood in the far corner, as tall as Josha and broader shouldered. He looked strong and lithe and his eyes were bright.

"I had to give him some of your clothes," Li explained excitedly.

"His was all torn up and bloody. Don't he look jist fine, Josha? He kin walk good, too. He still limps bad, but it'll git better. And there's a scar on his wrist, but thet'll git better too. You want to see him walk?"

Josha wanted to put a stop to Li's rambling, but didn't know how to go about it. Ezekiel did it for him. He opened his mouth and stammered, "Ma-ma-machine."

"What's he say?" Josha asked.

"He said machine," Li answered. "He's been sayin' thet all the time you been gone. I don't know what he means."

"Ma-chine," Ezekiel said.

Josha rubbed his beard and the silence in the cabin was overpowering. He could feel the wanting in Ezekiel. The man wanted to be understood.

"What is it?" Josha asked, approaching him within arm's reach.

Ezekiel strained, the muscles in his neck tense, his fists clenched. He closed his eyes and his mouth formed the words slowly. "Go — where — machine. Go machine."

"You know what he wants?" Li asked.

"He want to know what happened to his machine. He probably wants to see it."

"Go machine," Ezekiel repeated.

"Now?" Josha asked him. There was no response.

"Oh, not now," Li protested. "I don't think he kin make it on thet leg."

"If he wants to go now, we'll go now. I kin show him the way slow, Maybe seein' the machine will make him feel better." Josha held out his hand to Ezekiel. "Come. We'll go — where — machine, now."

The man hesitated for only a moment, then took Josha's hand and limped beside him through the door. The way was long and Josha went slowly, stopping every few yards to rest; he had to support Ezekiel most of the way.

When they reached the place where the machine stood tilted into the air, Ezekiel stopped and looked at it quietly for long moments. Then he started forward again, motioning that he wanted to be boosted through the door. Josha obliged and remained on the ground, tilting his head to watch.

Ezekiel limped to the chair, sat down, and began turning knobs and pressing buttons. Once when he pressed a button a little light appeared above it, but that was the only button which worked. The other lights remained dark.

Ezekiel growled and pounded his fists into the rows of knobs. Josha stepped back a pace. He saw Ezekiel bend over the knobs intently, link two small pieces of wire together and fasten the ends in different places along the wall. His face was visible when he turned to reach for wire and clippers, and Josha recognized something new in his eyes. Whether he could speak or not, the man was intelligent. Li was wrong; he was a foreigner.

Ezekiel dropped to the ground and pulled Joshua away from the machine, traveling as fast as his leg would allow. His anxiety carried Josha along in his wake. They hurried through the trees; then, without warning, Josha was thrown off his feet by a great gust of silent wind that plowed in from behind. Trees bent above him and bushes lashed at the ground. He cried out, but the sound was swallowed by the monster wind.

It passed as quickly as it had come, but Josha waited a long time before he moved. When he sat up, Ezekiel was standing beside him, looking back toward the machine. He limped away and Josha followed.

If the wind was frightening, the sight that met his eyes where the machine should have been was more so. There was nothing — no machine, no trees, no brush. Just a big, pure clearing that had been devoured — a huge circle of bare earth, not a blade of grass to break it. Ezekiel was smiling.

Josha knew now that he had to report Ezekiel in the little town; he had to get him out of their woods.

*****

The next morning when the dog returned from his jaunt into the woods, there was no cooking smell to greet him and no call to answer his excited barks. He trotted into the cabin, sniffing the air. He walked over to Li and poked her with his nose. She didn't stir. He went to Josha and scratched at the floor around him, whimpering high in his throat. Josha didn't move. An odor came strong from around them; it lay in the wet pools by their heads.

The dog tried once more to rouse them, then instinct told him it was no use. He crouched to his belly and bayed, creeping to the door and across the clearing. As the brush closed over him, he straightened and took off at a fast lope up the hill toward the warm, alive smell of Luke and Min.

CHAPTER FOUR

Letty Mason looked up from weeding the vegetable garden. The children were coming across the field waving their empty lunch sacks and the books cinched on the ends of straps. She pushed herself up from her knees.

They went to the house together, babbling about the sun and the teacher and whether the dog had missed them. It was a ritual Letty Mason never missed. When the children came back to her from school, they all had cookies and milk together in the warm kitchen and she listened while they read to her from their books.

She knew that his reading was making them grow away from her, but she wanted them to read. Tommy was almost good enough to read his father's books already. Soon she would hear the end of the one her husband had never been able to finish.

The children gulped their milk, wiped away their white mustaches, and rinsed their glasses as Letty set the pot to simmer on the wood stove. She was proud. She had been afraid when Charley died that it would be too much for her, but the bright eyes and clean faces around her proved that it wasn't.

"I've got a surprise for you," she called.

"A chocolate cake for supper," Tommy cried.

"A new swing," Sue guessed.

"No, it's bigger than that." They gathered around her and stared at her face. "Give up?" she asked. "I've saved enough money from last year's crop to hire me a man for around the place."

"A man!" Tommy shouted.

"He can fix the swing!" Sue wiggled up and down. Having a man about meant something different to each one of them, but it was a happy difference.

"Mostly, he can work so we can have more time together. I've left word with Mr. Goodall that I want a man, and he'll send anybody out who comes by. It'll be a blessing, I tell you."

Whatever she would have added was drowned in a baleful howl from far back at the wooded edge of the fields. It was repeated twice more before Tommy yelled, "That's Shep! He's in trouble!"

Letty caught the boy's sleeve as he darted for the door. "No, Tommy. Don't go out there. Not if he's howling like that."

"But, Ma, he may be hurt. I've gotta see."

"I guess we'll all go," Letty decided.

They were part way into the cabbage patch when Shep broke out of the woods and bounced gaily into the pasture. A man's figure stepped out of the trees, a tall man who limped toward them.

"Stay by me, children," Letty warned.

As the man neared, Letty appraised him closely. His clothes were plain and homely; he carried nothing in his hands. He raised his hand in greeting. Behind her, Letty heard a hiss and saw the cat head off for the barn, its tail puffed large and a growl inside its body.

"Did you want something special?" Letty asked, a little afraid because the man was a stranger and his eyes were so dark.

"I come to work. They told me in the town to come here."

"Oh." Letty relaxed, smiling. "Of course. I didn't expect anyone so soon." She suddenly couldn't think of what to say, but managed shyly. "Do you know anything about my kind of farming? Vegetables, and feed for our two cows?"

"I'm good at learnin' things," he answered. "You jist show me and I'll learn all thet quick."

The children tittered under their breaths and Letty flushed. The man was obviously just in from the hills. She hurried to cover for them: "It's not a great deal of pay, you know; but there will be good food and a warm place to sleep. You look strong enough, and the dog already likes you — I mean, I always sort of go by how a dog acts toward a person. Animals can tell, you know."

"Yup, they kin tell."

"I'm the Widow Mason; and these are my little ones, Sue and Tommy. Say, 'How do you do,' children."

The children smiled and repeated the words. Sue tried a shy curtsy. "What's your name?" Letty asked.

"I'm called Ezekiel."

"Ezekiel!" Letty turned the word on her tongue. "That's from the Bible, isn't it? My husband used to read me about Ezekiel from the Bible. What's your other name?"

"I ain't go no other name. Jist Ezekiel."

"Oh? Well, Ezekiel's good enough. If you want the job, you just come along to the house now and I'll show you where you can sleep. Do you have any things?"

"Nope, I ain't got nothin'. Jist myself."

Letty led the way to the house and the man limped behind her.

She took him to the extra room, gave him towels and bedding and left him alone. She should have asked him to help her finish the chores, but the stairs had made his limp worse.

*****

The next morning, Letty Mason started Ezekiel working and was pleased with him. She showed him what to do and he did it. He was a quiet man with little to say, retiring to his room immediately after supper. He had such a lonely look that Letty made up her mind to invite him to stay downstairs with them the next night.

She was glad for the way the children — and Shep — took to him. And even the cows gave extra milk for him. The only dissenter was old Puss, but she was a cat and Letty had never trusted cats too far. At first, while Shep bounded along beside Ezekiel, Puss hissed and skittered away; but by the end of the second day, she no longer ran but sat stock still, staring with round, yellow eyes. He kept his eye on her, too; and once Letty discovered them behind the barn, looking hard and silently at each other.

"What are you doing, Ezekiel?" she asked.

"Jist lookin' at the creature. I ain't never seen one them afore. There weren't none back — home."

"You've never seen a cat?" Letty was dumbfounded.

The cat's eyes never left Ezekiel's face, and his black ones gleamed at her. "She looks like she knows somethin', don't she?" Ezekiel murmured. "Like she kin see straight through you."

"Sometimes cats seem that way, but it's just nonsense."

Ezekiel didn't appear to have heard. He was still staring at the cat, his brow furrowed. "Come here, Puss," he coaxed, sticking out his hand. "Here, cat." The calm tone of his voice didn't match the intentness of his face. Puss didn't move or blink an eye. She crouched there, feet curled in under her fluffy chest, and glowered.

"What did you want fer me to do next?" Ezekiel faced away from the cat. "The sun's gittin' on."

*****

It was three days before Letty could convince Ezekiel to stay downstairs with them in the evening. The children were busy with their schoolwork, and she shyly tried to open a friendly conversation with the tight-mouthed man.

"You come from way back in the hills, don't you?" she asked. "Do your people live there?"

"I ain't got no people."

"I think it's a good idea for a man like you to get out of there. From what I've heard, there's no future for anybody living in the hills."

"There ain't. And as fer as I kin see, there ain't no future anywhere."

Letty glanced to her children, their heads bent over their books, fingers clutching pencils with stubby erasers and short points. "There's always something you don't know, no matter how long you live. I don't know much. My husband, he knew a lot of things; and it was all because he was educated. When he died and left me these two little ones, I promised that they were going to be educated. That's why I've worked so hard alone all these years."

Ezekiel followed her gaze and set his eyes on the children. He watched their pencils move across the paper and their eyes inch along the lines in the books. "What are they doin'?"

"That's their schoolwork. They're learning to read and write, do sums, and spell. Can you read and write, Ezekiel?"

"Nope, I guess I can't, if thet's what they're doin'."

Letty pressed Tommy's hand to stop him from writing. "Read something to Ezekiel, Tom; he can't read for himself." She smiled at the tall man. "I'm right proud of them. They're both as smart as whips."

Tommy lifted the book and began reading. The words came out evenly and well, describing a time in history when there were kings in the world and armies of men and horses.

Ezekiel listened, entranced. Tommy's voice droned on and on. Letty wanted to stop him after a while, but the expression on Ezekiel's face wouldn't let her. She knew the look well. It was hunger of the deepest kind — hunger for knowledge you never knew existed until someone opened the way for you.

When Tommy stopped of his own accord, Ezekiel took the book, scanning the page. "You got all thet from here?" he asked. "You know how to make sense of these here figures?"

"Sure he does," Sue answered.

Ezekiel cradled the book as though it were fragile. "How long does it take to know how to do it?"

"It's taken Tommy four years up till now," Letty stated.

"Four years." Ezekiel rose and paced to the door, the limp more noticeable in his excitement.

There was a sudden tenseness in the man's back; and Letty asked, concerned, "Is there anything wrong, Ezekiel?"

"Nope," his voice was soft but determined. "I jist realized there is somethin' more — somethin' I don't know."

*****

Ed Johnson drove up and honked his horn. Letty would explode out of the house with his eggs and then wait until he coaxed her to tell him about the hired man. He knew she had one, but he would never say so until she told him.

He honked again. As the noise died away, another sound caught his ears. Deep in the barn, the cows were mooing. They shouldn't be in the barn, they should be milked and out to pasture. He climbed out of the old car, his step quick. Something must be wrong. He hurried to the back door, knocked, and went in without waiting.

What he saw made him grab backward at the door for support. "My God! My God!" he cried.

He clutched his stomach, but he couldn't force his eyes from the scene. Letty lay on the floor, her head splattered in a circle of blood, a gaping hole in her skull. Tom and Sue were bent over the table, heads down, Sue's hair transformed from blond to terrible red. Tommy's blood spread across a map of Europe in a geography book.

Ed raced out the door. Someone had to help.

*****

The sun slipped low in the west as Bob and Linda Babcock sat on their front porch. It would soon be over for the summer. The last school bell would ring and the last blackboard would be washed. No more reports or teachers' meetings. No more secrecy about the expected baby. But the world would still be there and money would still have to be made.

"So if you want a flower garden again this year," Bob was saying, "you'll have to find somebody else to help you. I can't work six days a week and run a garden, too."

"I know. But should we give up the acre? We'll miss the vegetables."

"No, we've got to keep that. By fall we'll have the baby and we'll need it. I figure we can hire somebody part time. Joe thinks he has a man for his acre now. He said he'd send him over one of these days."

"I'm glad you see it that way." Linda touched his hand.

They didn't notice the sound of hard soles hitting the sidewalk along their street until a figure turned onto their walk.

Bob stood. "What can I do for you?"

"Joe Benson sent me. I take care of his garden, and he said maybe you'd be wanting somebody."

"Come on up, won't you?" Bob motioned to a seat on the glider. The stranger sat down, his eyes resting for a tiny second on Linda. "We were just talking about the garden, as a matter of fact. Do you think you could handle both jobs?"

"I figure I could." The man's voice was resonant and deeply entrenched in a drawl. Bob thought he probably had just come from Tennessee.

"I suppose I don't have to ask for qualifications," Bob smiled. "I mean, pulling weeds, and —"

"I got qualifications," the man said. "I worked on a farm and I can read and write."

Linda met her husband's glance. There was pity in it for a man who would say a thing like that. Especially a handsome man whose black eyes gleamed with so much latent intelligence.

"I can't pay much," Bob continued. "Just enough for a couple days' work a week."

The man nodded.

"Well, then, it's a deal," Bob said.

"Would you like a glass of iced coffee, Mr. —?" Linda added her voice.

"My name's Ezekiel, Ma'am."

"Ezekiel?"

"Like in the Bible."

Linda poured the coffee. She didn't really know why she had offered the drink. The man was a stranger, and peculiar. But there was something about him that made her want him to stay.

"I've heard about you folks," Ezekiel offered on his own. "Joe Benson has been talking about how you two know most everything there is to know about the world."

"Well, now," Bob said, chuckling, "we're not all that good. We're teachers. I teach geometry and trig, and Linda teaches history. On the side, I try to keep abreast of the news."

"Geometry? Trig?"

"Higher mathematics," Bob answered, but when there was still no understanding in the other's eyes, he added, "Arithmetic — higher arithmetic."

"It must be good to know so much."

Bob was uncomfortable with the conversation and turned it back to business. Ezekiel didn't mind the abrupt change and asked, "If you don't mind. I'd like some pay in advance. I ain't got any money right now, and I'll need a place to stay."

"I'll come in with you," Ezekiel said. He picked up the tray, following into the house after the two young people. It wasn't long before he came out and limped down the street.

When Joe Benson called later, there was no answer. The phone rang in a quiet house.

PART TWO

A new world is a disturbing place without understanding, and before understanding must come the materials for it. He had made a beginning — only a beginning. Turbulence inside his mind told him it was nothing more than that. Somewhere there was another mind that could quiet the turbulent places, that could release his own personal self by providing the understanding. He would know when he had found it.

CHAPTER FIVE

There were some places in the shady university town that nestled near the state capital where people still mourned the death of Professor Grayson. Assistant Head of the School of Psychology, he had had no personal enemies; only friends, disciples, and more than a few dissenters.

Even his most ardent disciple, Ray Harper, couldn't understand some parts of the professor's teachings and he had spent long evenings arguing with him.

Ray sat in his cubbyhole office and went over the latest results on his experiments. The August air was heavily hot and he couldn't concentrate, but it didn't matter. Aggression in rats was aggression in rats; nothing significantly new had shown itself in three years of work.

He glanced at his watch and wondered how soon Will would arrive. After five years, they would finally see each other again.

Two months before, when Will's letter had become filled with comments on the murder stories, Ray had grown uneasy. They reconjured memories he had steadfastly tried to suppress until a time when the hurt wouldn't be so strong.

As Will's letters kept coming, filled with his trip south to visit the sites of the murders, Ray had grown excited. Here, perhaps, was a chance to act, an opportunity to do something rather than sit back and dread opening the paper for fear there would be another murder story spread across it. There had been three since Professor Grayson, and no promise that a truce had been called.

Ray wondered momentarily if the years would have changed Will. His own mirror said probably not, because the years hadn't done anything to him. Perhaps he had a few more almost imperceptible lines, a bit more substance in his midsection, filling out; but his brown hair was still wavy and his face still angular with the same blue-ice eyes.

The rap at the door startled him, and he called, "Come in," rising to meet Will Purdom. They clasped hands strongly. Ray was newly amazed to see how close Will's head came to touching the door top.

"Don't ask me why I'm late," Will smiled. "This is a big campus and your directions weren't too clear."

Will arranged himself in the one available chair. The man hadn't filled out at all. Raw-boned and nearly skinny, he managed to radiate a sense of relaxation, every muscle long and easy. His brown eyes held the warmth that was saved for the people he liked. He opened the conversation easily: "This is a nice town, Ray. It's pure paradise after the places I've just seen."

"You like the 'Ivory Tower' atmosphere?" Ray asked.

"Sure, I like it. Don't ask me to stay too long; I might take you up on it."

"What about your job?"

"I've quit the paper," Will answered firmly. "I'm going out on my own, as a serious writer. I've had enough reporting — except for this murder story, which I want."

"Then you can stick around here." Ray was pleased.

"I intend to for a while anyway. If I'm going to work with you, I've got to be where you are."

"Work with me?"

"What do you think my letters have been about? My head's full of details and I want you to sort them out for me. I figure if anyone would have theories about murder, it would be you. Or have you given it up?"

"No, not given it up," Ray admitted. "I still keep my records. Maybe it's a morbid hobby, but I keep hoping that I'll come up with enough background to understand murder as such and maybe even prevent it."

"Well, I've dug up a couple of angles," Will Purdom said, "and we'll start from there." He drew out a pencil ready to take notes. "Now, tell me about Grayson so I can finish out my list, and then I'll fill you in on what I've found."

Ray sat back in the chair. "What do you want to know?"

"I'm trying to establish some link between the victims. I figure it has to be something unique, because I've tried every other angle like occupation, position — even robbery is out, since only the last few victims were robbed. I'm looking for personalities, eccentricities, hobbies — anything that might tie in. Did Grayson do anything especially unusual?"

Ray wrinkled his forehead, thinking back. "That's a hard question, Will, because he was interested in everything. You name it, and he knew something about it. He was that kind of man. A fine man. The best I knew in the world." Ray looked at the floor. "I practically lived at his house. He taught me most of the things I know — the things that aren't in textbooks. He was brilliant, crotchety, and gentle. That's the best description of him I can give you."

"What about the telepathy angle — the parapsychology?"

"We don't talk about that in this department. Professor

Grayson had a reputation that must be preserved. Parapsychology isn't considered science, and Grayson can't defend himself."

"That's real snobbery, isn't it?" Will shook his head. "Skip it now. What was he doing in Indiana?"

"He had just begun his sabbatical year and wanted a change of scene. He planned to stay a month, fishing and relaxing. He had only been gone two weeks when we got word."

"And, of course, you didn't see the body," Will stated.

"None of us did. He'd been dead for a few days when they found him, and his head was battered. They closed the coffin."

"Just like the other sixteen victims," Will sighed heavily. "Sixteen unrelated people. Farmers, schoolteachers, a writer, a playboy, a state senator, a professor. No motive and no decent description of the killer."

"No description at all, you mean," Ray corrected.

"Well, they know he's tall, if you can call that a description," Will offered. "There were people who were close to him when the senator was killed, and they know he wasn't wearing a hat and that he's about six feet tall. If we're dealing with a madman, he's a clever one, Ray." Will rubbed his nose. "Some of the things I've found out puzzle me. For instance, all of these murders just happened. There was no warning, no anything. The victims died with no struggle. The Mason woman's children were found bent over their schoolbooks; the senator had finished half a highball; the preacher's wife was reading her Bible, her husband beside her. What did it?"

"A blow on the head, according to the examiners. It doesn't exactly jibe, does it?"

"No, because a blow on the head could only kill one at a time. And I saw pictures, Ray — pictures of the dead people. Their skulls weren't just cracked open; they were exploded! As though they had been pushed — from the inside."

"Now, wait a minute," Ray cut in. "You're getting too far out. A blow on the head could give the impression you're describing. Let's not make this more mysterious than it is."

"All right," Will said, surrendering. "You lead the way. But I'm warning you; it won't be long until you're right back with me."

Will drew out a small map and spread it on the desk. "This is pretty flimsy, but look. Here's where the first murders were committed — in Tennessee. That was the Mason woman and her two kids. Draw a line from there to the second murder and you get the tip end of Kentucky. The next one was in southern Illinois. He stayed around Illinois for a while; but the pattern is there, north and a little east. From Illinois he went to southern Indiana. He'd been hitting simple people up until then; but in Indiana he picked off Grayson, the senator, and the rich kid. He's changed the class of victim, but he's still moving north and east."

"I see what you mean," Ray mused, "if he's not through, then he either slipped into Ohio or Michigan."

"Ohio is too far east. I think he came into Michigan, and that puts him somewhere near us."

"Michigan's a big state."

"Nothing's big when you've got a lunatic loose in it."

Ray drew out a cigarette and lit it. "You said you couldn't find any motives or even connection between the victims?"

"*I* couldn't, but you're a psychologist and you've studied murder for years. Maybe you can turn up something."

"It will have to be spare time."

"That's all I can give it myself."

"Then it's a deal." Ray clapped him on the back. "We'll put our heads together and see what happens. Right now, I've got a dinner date with Carol Grayson. Want to come along?"

"What will she say? She's never met me."

"She'll like you. And she always cooks enough for an army."

The August air was oppressive in the corridors; but outside, under the elms, it was better.

"You've still got your mind on the murders, Will," Ray commented as they proceeded along a shaded walk. "I thought we put that aside for the day."

"Sorry," Will muttered. "But I can't ever get it entirely off my mind since I found out one other thing about the victims — something that isn't public knowledge. They all did have one other thing in common: *All of their brains were withered!*"

*****

Carol Grayson's house wasn't far — a short way down the shady street that lay around the campus. The house was white, old, and boxy, surrounded by bright beds of asters and zinnias which Carol had babied all summer.

As Ray Harper and Will Purdom reached the porch, something stirred in the bushes and Mr. Chips appeared, blinking in the sun. He stopped momentarily to stretch his furry front legs, then thrust his striped tail in the air and trotted up the steps to Ray.

Ray picked up the cat and pushed the doorbell. Carol answered immediately, looking more like a young housewife, with her hair pulled back into a ponytail, than a twenty-five-year-old Master of

Arts.

"Look who I found," Ray laughed. "An official welcoming committee." He held up one of the cat's paws and Carol took it in her hand, bending to bury her face in Mr. Chips soft chest.

"Where have you been, Tiger?" she asked. The cat started to purr and Ray felt the vibrations through his hands. Then Carol's hazel eyes were on Will, and her eyebrows raised.

"This is Will Purdom, Carol. I've told you about him."

"Oh, really? That Will?" Carol's voice was genuinely pleased. "I'm glad to meet you — finally." Will shook Carol's hand and scratched Chips under the chin, and Carol asked, "Do you like cats?"

"Yes, indeed," Will answered.

"Then welcome to our house. Chips says welcome, too, don't you, Tiger?" Chips rubbed his head on her hand.

Carol led the way to the living room, Will's eyes following her easy walk, noting the way the blue cotton skirt swished about her bare legs. Carol's face was gentle and well-formed, framed in silken brown hair. Her eyes, set wide and clear, sparkled with a sense of frankness and intelligence.

"I hope dinner's on," Ray commented. "I'm starved."

"It's all on but the salad. If you'll give Chips his dinner, I'll set another place at the table."

"Come on, Will," Ray called. Will followed through the comfortable rooms, rather like a lost sheep trailing in Ray's wake. "We don't stand on ceremony in this house," Ray explained as he set Chips on a chair. "When Carol says a person is welcome, she means just that."

"She's a beautiful girl, Ray."

All through dinner, Will watched the pair across from him. There was something between them that he could sense.

With the steaming after-dinner coffee in the living room, the conversation turned to the reason Will had come. With the mention of her father's death, Carol's face twisted in a momentary flash of pain, but she said, "I don't think you'll find much to go on here. It's been two months now, and the police asked me all of the questions."

"I certainly don't want to bother you with any more," Will said earnestly. "I didn't intend to ask you about it."

"I don't shy away from discussing it. I just don't dwell on it. It's done and whoever is responsible is insane — that much I know — and you can't take revenge on a madman."

"There is one thing I would like to know, Carol," Will said suddenly. "I've heard that your father was interested in telepathy, more or less as a hobby."

"Not as a hobby," she stated firmly. "If it had been possible, telepathy would have been my father's main work. He believed in it — entirely. And he had the proof to back it up."

"I asked Ray the same question this afternoon, but he wouldn't admit it."

"He wouldn't," Carol laughed. "Poor Ray is afraid. It wouldn't fit the pattern of the 'experimentalist' he's trying to build for himself. But he read all of Dad's notes. See, my father was trying to establish all the possible kinds of ability — telepathy, clairvoyance, teleportation. He had quite a few subjects here that he used. Some of them pretty good, too. He always wanted to work with Ray," she laughed, teasing, "but he was too hard-nosed to consent."

"Ray? A telepath?" Will laughed with her.

"Not really a telepath," Carol explained. "But Ray made the mistake of admitting that he gets certain feeling about people — about their emotions underneath the surface — and Dad never let him live it down. It's simply that he knows what a person is, no matter what they've made other people think they are."

Ray scowled at them and went over to pet Mr. Chips, who reclined lazily in an easy chair. "Would you stop talking about me as if I weren't here?" he said. "Now that you know my secret, all I ask is that you keep it secret."

"I rely on Chips," Carol's eyes were warm on the cat. "He's not afraid to admit that he knows about people. The person Chips doesn't like, I don't like. But mostly it's the person who doesn't like Chips that I avoid. He hasn't failed me."

Chips looked up at his name, his golden eyes closing tight in a Cheshire smile, his front feet curling into firm balls, one at a time.

When the grandfather's clock struck eleven, Will made polite good-bys and went to the car, leaving the two for a moment by themselves. Carol walked to the door with Ray. "I like your friend, Ray. He's all you've said and a little more. Is he going to stay?"

"I think so, if we can introduce him around and make him feel at home."

She placed her hands on his shoulders. "Why don't you invite him along to May's party next week?" As Ray drew back a bit, she caught him tighter. "No, now don't protest. I want to go to that party. May's phoned me three times this week, telling me all about this new man she's found."

"I know. Tall, dark and handsome — immensely interesting and overwhelmingly fascinating. When will May grow up?"

"Don't begrudge her the little she's got," Carol chided. "I gather this man's a politician. Anyway, I want to see him."

"You win." Ray drew her close. "I'll invite Will and we'll all have a look."

CHAPTER SIX

The night was so close to being hot that even the moonlight held a warmth. It was late for the start of a party, but May Randle wanted it that way. She paraded her talents best in halflight; and as Ray stepped onto Carol's porch, he sighed with resignation, knowing full well what kind of a night lay in store.

May would display her new friend as though he were her own creation, hovering and passing drinks in the grand house until her gushing became unbearable.

Ray was surprised when he saw Carol. He was always surprised when she dressed that way, transforming herself from the lithe, wholesome girl of the day into a dark-haired siren. She seemed to wrap a cloak of ladyhood about her and emerged from the ponytail regal and elegant.

As they drove the quiet streets to May's house, Carol kept up a stream of chatter, explaining to Will about the people he would meet. "Don't be frightened because they're mostly psychologists. They're off work and not about to analyze anybody."

Will laughed from the back seat, where he had gathered his long frame into an uncomfortable hump. "Is May really as nutty as you make her sound?"

"No," Carol chided. "She's all right. The campus wouldn't be the same without her. She's alone, that's all, and has too much money. She did a stint in silent movies and got so steeped in the 'big show' that she does everything that way."

They drove through the gate and up a winding drive to a big stone house and Will understood. The front yard glowed with Japanese lanterns strung between fancy lamp posts. Behind the lights the house sprawled with a certain elegance that had once been dignity. Behind it was a formal garden leading out to three acres of grounds.

Each step toward the house brought voices and music to a louder pitch. The house itself was dimly lit; and three people materialized from the shadows as Carol, Ray and Will went onto the porch. Carol made hurried introductions. The only name Will remembered was Margaret Horton, and that was because she was dressed in red.

They were barely inside when a flash of whirling chiffon descended on them, and May Randle gathered in her belated guests. She was all fluffy and fancy with grey-yellow hair and a cloud of perfume that engulfed everyone within three feet. Will took her thin hand gallantly and responded with his best formality. He obviously passed the test, for May led him around, introducing one person after another until Will's head reeled.

When he could, Will crossed the small dance floor to rejoin Ray and Carol. They were ensconced at a little bar. He made himself a tall drink and sat down. "I never imagined faculty parties could be so lively."

"The department head isn't here," Carol explained. "Everyone can let his hair down and be happy."

"Well, then, as soon as I finish this drink, I'm going to ask you to dance, Miss Carol."

May's perfume announced her coming before she reached them. Carol stopped her as she fluttered by and gave vent to her curiosity. "Where's the new man, May? Couldn't he make it?"

"Haven't you met him yet?" May squinted around the dim room. "He hasn't come back in, I suppose. He went out for some air." She leaned close to Carol. "I'll bring him over just as soon as he comes. He's fascinating, dear, simply marvelous."

Someone called and May scurried away. "That's quite a gal," Will said. "She must have been a beauty."

The noise of the party droned on, then lessened abruptly. Ray looked up and say that Carol's eyes were focused across the room, resting on a man who had just come through the garden door.

There are some people who can be in a room for hours and never be noticed. This was not one of them. This man walked in with such authority that without a word everyone knew he was there.

Ray eyed him casually, but Carol couldn't take her attention from him. She watched as he moved among the guests. Most of the people leaned toward him to catch his words; but with some of the guests there was an opposite reaction — a drawing away, and a nervousness.

Then May appeared beside the man and brought him toward the bar. Carol straightened, pushing her shoulders back, waiting for his glance to fall upon her.

The man walked stiffly, the hesitancy centered in his left leg as though it could be a definite limp if he relaxed. Ray's first impression was one of aloofness — something held off and away. It radiated from the man's high head and arched brows. It was obvious right away that he was somebody. "Well," Ray murmured, "May's really gone all out this time."

Carol didn't answer. She felt a strange sense of anticipation that clutched her stomach and encircled her body. By the time the man reached her, she had studied every feature of him: the solid height, the broad-set face, the black hair — everything about him just a touch off-beat. And his eyes were black — dark to the core. They penetrated her with a glow that came from deep inside. She heard May's voice dimly as she raised her hand to take his.

"Carol, this is Peter Kiel. I've told him about you, dear. Peter, this is Carol Grayson."

Carol's hand was clasped in a warm, strong grip. Then the eyes were gone, focusing on Ray and Will; and she picked up her glass, self-conscious for one of the first times in her life.

He was speaking with Ray. She realized that Ray was being quite reserved and thought briefly that he was foolish because those eyes could see inside him and know what he was holding back.

Then Will's touch brought her out of the daze; and as she moved away to dance with him, she realized with fright that she had been lost for those few moments.

Will felt her shiver. "What's wrong, Carol? You can't be cold."

"No," she hesitated, "I just had the strangest experience." She couldn't explain it, so she brushed it aside. "I suppose I'm still not quite myself, and the noise got to me — I mean, since Dad — I haven't been much of anyplace."

"Do you want some air?"

"Yes, please. We can go into the garden."

They danced around to the door and stepped out into the freshness. Carol sat down on a stone bench and pulled her flimsy stole about her shoulders. She didn't speak, and Will let long minutes pass before he asked, "Better now?"

"I'm fine." She dropped back to silence, then out of nothing, asked, "He's quite something, isn't he? No wonder May has called me so often." She abruptly turned the subject away. "Ray's going to wonder where we've gone. Do you suppose you'd better let him know?"

"Do you want to be alone? Is that what you're trying to say?"

"I think so — for a few minutes. Leave me a cigarette?"

Will handed her his pack and lighter and left without protest. Carol remained on the bench. The sounds of the party were faintly distant, and there was just enough light to see the smoke rise from her cigarette.

The voice startled her, coming from close behind. "I see you've escaped, too."

She turned quickly to stare into the strong features of Peter Kiel. "Escaped?"

"The party — the noise and smoke. It's quite oppressive." He sat down in Will's place, drawing out a cigarette of his own.

"I like parties." Carol tried to fill the silence. "But tonight is too beautiful to waste inside. The moon's nearly full."

He followed her gaze to where the moon rested, white and flat-surfaced. "Yes, it won't be long."

Carol was uncomfortable in the silence and tried to find some common ground between them. "May said you are a politician, Mr. Kiel. Is that why you're here in the capital?"

"No, I don't hold an office. I'm just getting started. May exaggerates everything." He took a long puff on the cigarette, then amazed Carol by saying, "But she didn't exaggerate you. You're as beautiful as she said you would be."

She knew she should murmur, "Thank you" and turn away; but instead she looked at him squarely, head up. The black eyes held frankness and calm approval. "May told you about me, then?"

"Only because I asked her to find me a woman like you. I supplied requirements, and she chose you."

Carol did turn away at that. "You're very frank, Mr. Kiel. The way you put it, it sounds rather like supply and demand."

"It is rather like that," he said with no trace of a smile.

Carol felt strangely surrounded, as though what he said was undeniably true and there was no other way about it.

"Would you like to walk about a bit?"

They went between the rows of flowers and along the spotted grass. They spoke very little, but Carol found she didn't have to speak. An emotion she couldn't name enveloped her and made her close to the man who strode beside her. Magnetic, it reached out to wrap round and round her.

They made one circle of the grounds and she was willing to try another; but Kiel's stride had changed to one of slight hesitation, a halting at every step.

She faced him. "Does your leg hurt much? You're limping."

"It's nothing bad, but I think I will sit down."

"Let's go in then," she suggested.

He took her to the door; and just before they went in, he whispered, "Don't get lost from me in the crowd. Come back."

He went ahead as Carol waited to collect herself. The music touched her, muted and distant; and the figures of people swam in slow motion. Ray broke the spell, his face red and tight. "Where on earth have you been? I've looked all over for you."

"I'm sorry, Ray. I was talking to Mr. Kiel. I didn't feel well and —"

"Will told me. You're all right now, aren't you?"

She squeezed his hand. "Of course. I'm sorry I went off like that. I don't quite understand it myself. Let's have a drink. You must be way ahead of me."

They returned to the bar, where Will sat a bit too close to a friend, Margaret Horton, talking intently about the death of Professor Grayson. When Carol neared, the conversation stopped.

Ray growled at Will: "I should think you'd know better. That's no conversation for a party in the first place."

"Don't be that way," Carol protested. "I'm not going to live the rest of my life in a shell. If they want to talk about murders, let them."

Whatever she would have added was drowned in the gush of May's voice. Two professors were arguing rat psychology in the corner and wanted Ray to referee. He went reluctantly, disappearing behind the dancers and the smoke.

"You stayed away pretty long, Carol," Will chided gently.

"I was talking to Mr. Kiel," she said defensively.

"I don't blame you," Maggie laughed. "That's what I call having a real party. I've tried to corner that man three times tonight and gotten nowhere."

Carol let her eyes wander about the room. "Who is your date tonight, Maggie?"

"Ralph. Why?"

"Because he's trying to get your attention. Hadn't you better see what he wants?"

Maggie sauntered away and Will poured more liquid into Carol's glass. "What *do* you think of May's friend?"

"If I'm honest, you'll think I'm terrible," Carol blushed.

"What does that mean?"

"Simply that Maggie described him perfectly. He's quite a person. So different you'd hardly believe he was real."

"Ray doesn't like him." Will's bluntness was almost unkind.

"Ray doesn't know him."

"He met the man and talked to him. You told me that Ray's feelings about people are usually right, Carol. He has strong feelings about Peter Kiel."

"What did he say?" Carol's voice was too lacking in curiosity to be genuine.

"He couldn't put it exactly. It's just that he think Kiel is wary —

that he's calculating. I had pretty much the same response. He meets you square on, and then suddenly you're beneath him without his saying one word. It's as if he measured you, judged you, and cast you aside. If that sounds foolish, maybe it's just the liquor."

"Let's say it's the liquor. You're both wrong." She pressed one hand to her head. "Something's wrong with this party, Will."

"It seems like a good party to me."

"Don't you feel the electricity in the air? The tension? I keep thinking I should be doing something, that something is going to happen."

"My thoughts, exactly." Ray spoke from behind her, then he sat down in Maggie's place. "It's a good thing you're not sensitive about it, Carol, because there are only two topics of conversation here tonight. Peter Kiel and the murders."

"You can't blame people for that," she said. "I'm probably more immune than anyone else. I've had the blow and I'm not afraid of it anymore. They still have to wait."

"You've hit it square," Will aid. "These murders are personal to everybody. No one can say, 'I don't need to worry,' because no one knows that he won't be next."

Carol was engrossed in the talk; and when a hand touched her shoulder, she swiveled, frightened, to meet the face of Peter Kiel. "Oh, it's you," she cried in relief. "This murder talk is as bad as a ghost story."

"I thought perhaps I'd join you." He looked to Ray and Will. "If you don't mind?" he added.

"Not at all," Will answered for them all. "Sit down. We were just discussing some theories about the murders."

"You, too?" Kiel said with a sigh. "And do you have any theories?"

"Not really," Ray admitted. "We're working on them."

"I should have suspected it." Kiel's glance swung to Carol. "It's rather close to you, isn't it? I understand that the Professor Grayson who was killed was your father."

"Yes, he was," Carol murmured.

"I'm sorry. "There was none of the soft sympathy Carol had heard so often lately; it was just a statement. "I haven't followed the thing too closely, but I gather it's baffling everyone."

Ray couldn't account for the uneasy feeling that forced his fingers to drum on the side of his glass. "You sound rather as though it didn't baffle you. Do you have a theory?"

"No, not at all," Kiel answered. "I go along with the rest. It must be the work of a lunatic."

"Will doesn't think so," Ray continued. "He thinks there is a pattern; and if so, then a lunatic is out."

"A pattern?" The black eyes swerved to Will. "Where?"

"Ray is exaggerating. I haven't found a pattern, really. Just a direction."

"What are you talking about?" Carol asked impatiently.

Will pulled out a pencil and drew a rough-sketched map on a pink napkin, filling in the lines he had shown Ray. The point was obvious. The line had to continue to Michigan.

Peter Kiel saw it too. "That's very interesting. It hadn't occurred to me. If this is true, then the killer could very possibly be somewhere in this vicinity."

"That's why I'm here," Will answered. "It's morbid, but I want the story and I'm waiting for the next strike."

"The motive for the last murder, at least, was robbery, wasn't it?" Kiel said quietly.

"It might be, and it might not," Will answered. "The early victims had nothing worth stealing."

"But going on the assumption that the killer is not a lunatic, then he must have taken some profit from his victims. That brings up the interesting question of 'what?'"

Carol didn't like the turn the conversation had taken and she said, "But he *is* a lunatic and he simply took pleasure from the murders. The pleasure of seeing people's heads bashed in."

Kiel looked at her with appraisal. "This had gotten to be too much for you, hasn't it? Would you like to try the air again?"

"Yes, I'd like that. We won't be too long, Ray."

She stood beside Kiel and he took possession of her by the simple placing of one hand on her back to guide her.

Ray's mouth was open in surprise as Will chuckled, "Well, well, well. Fancy that."

"I don't fancy it at all," Ray growled.

"Don't get worked up. She's made the catch of the night and she's riding the waves."

"I never figured Carol would fall with the rest."

"You've got to admit he does present a puzzle."

"What puzzle?" asked Ray.

"Did you notice the way he looked when he dropped that little theory about the murders? As though he were saying 'I know the answer, and here's a crumb, stupid — now try to figure it out for yourself.'"

CHAPTER SEVEN

They stayed toward the back of the house where the lights from the blazing driveway wouldn't intrude. Carol strolled beside Peter Kiel and while they walked, she was comfortable; but when they sat down on the stone bench and she could think of nothing to say, it became uncomfortable.

Finally, she straightened and blurted: "You know, Mr. Kiel, if we're ever going to talk to each other, I've got to take myself in hand and get over being afraid of you."

"Afraid of me?" His eyes were bold on her, uncanny in their blackness.

She shook her head. "I can't explain it. I can't quite reach you — you seem so remote."

"That's a strange adjective."

"I know it is, but it comes naturally."

"Then we'll have to do something to get rid of it. If I told you that dogs and little children like me, would that make you feel better?"

She laughed, reddening. "You win. I take it back." She walked a short distance to a large shaft that pointed skyward from a cement base.

"What's that?" he asked, following.

"Another of May's luxuries — a telescope. Do you want to see the moon?" She adjusted the scope, trying to aim it at the sphere above their heads.

"Here, let me do it." He placed sure hands on the tube, one eye to the viewer; and brought the scope to bear on the craggy lunar surface. "You can't see any features; it's too bright," he explained, then joked: "But I don't see any Moonmen, either."

She moved up to see. "At least there aren't any eight-legged monsters," she laughed.

He stared at her, estimating. "There are other things besides appearance. How they *think* is the thing you should worry about. Do you think about monsters very often? It's an unlikely subject for a girl like you."

Carol rubbed her hand over the smoothness of the tube. "I guess I inherited it from my father. He had an insatiable curiosity, and the possibility of space creatures couldn't be left unturned just because people scoff at it."

"I understand that your father was a brilliant man," Kiel said casually. "He was interested in the sixth sense."

"Someone's been talking. That isn't common knowledge."

"How about a drive? I'd rather not go back to that party."

"It sounds wonderful."

Kiel propelled her to a gleaming length of metal which he proclaimed to be his car. He slid onto the seat beside her, chose a route back toward the campus, then bypassed it and headed for the river drive to Capitol City. The water was bright with moonlit ripples and circles that spread from willow branches dangling in shallows.

Kiel parked the car and they sat in silence, sharing the sight of the moon lowering itself over the countryside to the west of the city. Then Carol began to talk. She talked about herself, telling him things that she had kept secret from everyone but her father. He drew her out and she didn't feel strange, airing her life before a stranger. And to her approval he kept his hands fastidiously to himself.

Later, as they drove to her house, then walked up the path, she marveled at the way their relationship had changed from awkwardness to rapport.

The stillness was broken by the frightening bay of the spotted dog who was Chips's nemesis. He gave vent to a full-throated howl, and Carol reached for Kiel's hand. He took it absently. His brow creased as though concentrating on something, and then the bay changed to a friendly bark and the dog bounded out of the bushes to meet them.

Kiel bent to pet his speckled head, murmuring, "So the moon got the best of you, too, boy?"

"Don't make friends with him," Carol smiled. "He's the enemy." The dog wagged up to her, eagerly baleful. "Oh, you mutt," she scolded, petting him. "When you look like that, how can anyone help but forgive you?" She straightened. "We'd better not pet him anymore. He's going to wag his tail so hard it will fall off. Let's go in." She thrust her key into the lock. "Wait till you see my friend. He'll run to the door, and then pretend he doesn't care whether I'm home or not."

"I didn't know you had a pet."

"Didn't I tell you? I have a cat — Mr. Chips. " A fleeting change came over the tall man. "You do like cats, don't you?"

"Yes," he assured her. "I like cats very much. But — unfortunately, cats don't take to me."

"Nonsense," Carol scoffed, and pulled at his hand. He followed reluctantly and she laughed. Then she snapped on the lights and saw the end of Chips's inflated tail disappear around the living room arch and heard the echo of a hiss. "Well, for heaven's sakes. We must have frightened him."

"No," Kiel shook his head. "I told you cats don't like me."

"But not that violently, surely."

"That violently. And it's a funny thing, because I admire them. I've always wanted to get near a cat, but I've never been able to do it."

Carol was pulled two ways at that moment. Chips had told her point blank his feeling on the subject of Peter Kiel, and he had never been wrong. Still . . .

"Maybe it's your shaving lotion," she suggested, smiling weakly.

Something stirred near the living room door and two golden eyes peered at them from nearly floor level. Chips's brown ears were back and his tongue protruded from his lips. A soft growl escaped his chest. Carol picked him up unceremoniously.

"Tiger," she scolded, "do you think that's nice?" The cat didn't cease its growling.

"Don't get yourself scratched over it," Kiel urged.

"He won't scratch me," she answered surely, but she let the cat down. "We'll try him again the next time you come."

"Then there will be a next time?" Kiel asked.

"You didn't need to ask that question."

"I sensed a strong kinship between you and your cat and thought perhaps you'd take his word."

"This is one time I can judge for myself." And as Kiel turned, one hand on the knob, she added, "I know it's not proper, Peter; but — don't you want to kiss me good night?"

He touched her, ignoring the growling cat; and wrapped her in his arms, kissing her as though she were something fragile that might break apart.

*****

Time had bitten two weeks out of September when Will met Ray outside his last class. As the two men walked toward town, Will noted a new look about Ray — a pinched, angry look that was bitterness.

"What about the party Friday night?" Will asked. "Is she coming?"

"No," Ray answered with finality. "Not this Friday or any Friday, that I can see."

"Did she give any explanation?"

"She's busy. She's sorry, but she's busy."

"I don't believe Carol would put out a blunt excuse like that," Will said, bridling.

"Maybe I goaded her into it. Anyway, it's a simple case of in and out. Kiel's in and everybody else is out."

Ray recalled the snide remarks he'd been hearing in the department. Kiel had walked into their group and taken it over, dividing it unequally at about the three-quarter point. There were no bystanders where Kiel was concerned. People liked him wholeheartedly, almost to the point of worship, or they shrank from him. The people Ray valued most in the world were the ones who shrank.

The power of the man was fantastic. When he appeared, he was immediately surrounded; the climbers, the thrill-seekers, the somebodys or would-be somebodys flocked around him, hoping some of his influence or just some of "him" would rub off. And he manipulated them like a puppeteer — holding fast to the ones he wanted, sloughing the others off with remarks that shriveled them.

Will's words snapped Ray out of his musing. "Are you going to let Carol cut herself off? Leave her to face the wolf alone?"

"What else can I do? I talk and she doesn't hear one word. Normally, she wold have been one of the first to see through Kiel; but she's eating out of his hand. Maybe she's after the title of First Lady of the State — I don't know. I do know that all he needs to do is say the word and he'll be Governor."

"He doesn't strike me as a man in a hurry," Will answered quietly.

They crossed the street, dodging cars, and went into a drugstore. After a quick coffee, Ray left for Carol's house to pick up some notes. There was a hint of red and yellow in the tree leaves, and late flowers bloomed in their last flurry of color beside the white house.

Carol answered his ring lazily. She was so fresh and clean that she appeared to have just stepped from bed and a bath. Mr. Chips bounced up to rub against his legs, asking why he had stayed away so long. Ray picked him up and let him ride on his shoulders. When he sat down, the cat perched on his lap while Ray stroked his striped fur.

"I wish he'd be that way with Peter," Carol opened on a sour note. "I'd almost begun to think he was getting crotchety."

"You mean Chips and Kiel don't get along?"

"No, they don't. But it's all one sided. Peter likes Chips a lot, but Chips just sits and stares."

Ray scratched the tiger face under the chin, congratulating Chips for his good judgement. The cat suddenly stiffened in his hands and climbed to the back of the chair, where he gathered his feet under him and peered toward the kitchen. Ray followed his direction and found Peter Kiel.

"Hello," Kiel said, coming into the room, his limp more noticeable than before.

"You've done too much work today, Peter," Carol scolded. "You'd better sit down. He mowed the lawn for me," she explained to Ray. "Heavy work puts too much strain on his leg."

"What happened to your leg?" Ray asked.

"It was an accident, less than a year ago," Kiel answered. "It didn't heal well because of sheer stupidity."

"It was a pretty bad crash," Carol put in.

"I'm sorry," Ray added, wanting nothing more than to get away. He didn't like the way Kiel's eyes played across him.

"How are you coming with your murder theories?" Kiel asked. "Have you found any clues?"

"No, and I doubt I ever will," Ray said bluntly. "I've about given up, but Will plows on. He's stubborn."

"Peter's been reading over some of Dad's notes on telepathy," Carol said, opening a new subject when she saw that the present one was dry. "He's interested in animals, Ray. You two should combine."

Ray made no response, afraid of saying the wrong thing. Carol babbled on, telling him how much Kiel was like her father. Ray wondered why she was trying so hard, but decided to go along with her. "What is it that interests you in animals, Mr. Kiel? I don't get the connection."

"Peter calls it animal telepathy," Carol answered for him.

"Animal telepathy? That's rather farfetched, isn't it?"

"No, I don't think so." Kiel was ready to defend himself. "You can't deny a sixth sense in animals."

Ray pulled out a cigarette and said firmly: "The sixth sense in animals is instinct. A lost dog goes home by instinct just like a homing pigeon."

"I believe that is a popular fallacy," Kiel countered. "What about the cases where an animal has been left behind when its owner moved to a location the animal had never seen, and then the animal turned up there? How did he get there? Not instinct, by any stretch of the imagination."

"Then what was it?" Ray challenged. "Not telepathy."

The look of condescension that crossed Kiel's face was maddening. "It's really quite simple to deduce. The animal 'knew' where its people had gone and the only possible explanation for its knowing is that it 'sensed' them. You might say that it could follow them because it knew their brain patterns, just as it would know their spoor. And a brain wave, being like any other energy wave, travels. The animal caught the waves and homed in on them. And not only can they receive, they can send. They have their own pattern."

A bell rang in the kitchen and Carol hurried to answer it, mumbling something about burned cookies. Ray held his response until she was out of the room. "That presupposes that animals think," he threw back at Kiel. "You've gone too far."

"I didn't say 'thought' waves." Kiel's black eyes sought his and held fast. "I said 'pattern.' Animals can sense human patterns; and if a human being had the ability, he could just as easily sense the animal's patterns."

"And all of this," Ray said nastily, "boils down to a simple fact that you're trying to find out why Chips doesn't like you. Well, maybe he doesn't like the way you think."

"I should have expected that," Kiel said smiling. "You've been antagonistic from the first. Is a new idea too much for you?"

"Maybe not." Ray stood, confused by the anger he felt in himself. "I think I'll grant your theory, Mr. Kiel, because I believe I have some of the ability you're talking about. I can tell what Chips, here, is thinking — or feeling or sending — however you want it. He's sending pure, undiluted hate your way, isn't he? Not fright, just hate."

Kiel stiffened and leveled his gaze at Ray, then bit his lip and looked away. Ray felt an intense challenge directed toward him. But Carol's return with a dish piled high with cookies saved him from whatever that challenge might have been. But from Kiel's look, Ray knew it wasn't called off, just postponed.

CHAPTER EIGHT

Peter Kiel became impossible to avoid. It was either a matter of staying away from Carol or seeing them together.

The psychology department was full of romantic talk. Carol had her own opinions of the man, and they were unshakable. Ray winced every time he heard the adjectives Carol used in her comments — adjectives that never in the world should fit Peter Kiel. Gentleness was not a part of the man; neither was compassion, nor sensitivity. Yet those qualities were there for Carol.

Will tried to make Ray understand what he had seen between them. The two of them seemed to conjoin to fall together perfectly. It was as though Carol had become a part of Peter Kiel.

It was one day, when Ray had settled down to the busy work of preparing lectures, that Will burst into Ray's office with a letter in his hand. "My digging finally turned up a little piece of something," he bubbled. "Read this, Ray. It's the first definite thing we have to go on."

Ray glanced at the handwriting. It was scraggly and uneven. The postmark was from Tennessee. He took the letter from the envelope.

"It's from a Mr. Goodall — he runs a store in the town by the Mason woman's farm," Will explained. "I talked to people down there, but he wasn't around. Now he writes that he thinks he's the only man who got any sort of a look at the killer."

"Is there a good description?"

"Pretty good. Letty Mason wanted a farm hand and left word with Goodall. He sent one just a few days before she was killed. He's convinced that man was the killer. There was evidence on the farm that an extra person had been there."

"A hired man?" Ray mused. "Unskilled, then. Probably a farmer himself."

"Not much of anything, according to Goodall," Will said, shaking his head. "He says in the letter that he met the man on the road. He didn't get a real look at him; he just told him where the Mason farm was and that was it."

"But you said a description," Ray protested.

"He's tall and to the best of Goodall's recollection, dark-haired. The distinguishing thing about him is the fact that he has a thick mountain drawl. Goodall pegged him as a mountain man from Arkansas. That fits in with our directional pattern. He was still traveling northeast."

Ray lit a cigarette quickly, blowing out a billow of blue smoke. "That's a good help. A drawl like that shouldn't be too hard to spot up here."

"There's more." Will handed the information like an old woman with a juice piece of gossip. "Goodall's kids went to school with the Mason kids, and they talked about their hired hand a good deal. They remembered part of his name. Ezekiel."

Something squirmed in Ray's mind. "Didn't you say the preacher's wife had her Bible open to Ezekiel when she was killed?"

"Of course! That's the connection. She was reading from Ezekiel; as well as I can remember, they said it was the part about the vision of the wheels. It's too much to be coincidence."

"It isn't a coincidence," Ray stated flatly. "How did Goodall say he was dressed?"

"Work clothes — patched and dirty. And he thinks he remembers seeing a bandage on one of his hands."

"What about his behavior?" Ray asked the psychologist's question. "Was there anything unusual in that?"

"Only that he didn't say much. Goodall figured he was uneducated — as he says, just plain dumb."

Ray's face suddenly dropped back to its angular seriousness. "But where does this put us? So his name is Ezekiel and he's from Arkansas. We can't find him. Are you going to give this information to the police?"

"Naturally. They've got a better chance to use it than we have. But it's a glimmer of hope for me. I managed to turn this up; maybe more will come in."

"You can retrace all your steps," Ray agreed, "asking specifically for a man named Ezekiel. People might remember that. Anyway, you deserve congratulations; and to celebrate, I'll buy you a cup of coffee at the grill."

*****

The grill was crowded and dimmed by cigarette smoke that the fans couldn't eliminate. Maggie Horton waved from the far end of the room, alone at a table spread with papers, which she gathered into a bundle to thrust inside the pages of a book. Ray had just pulled up a chair when she began: "What do you think of the news?"

"I haven't head any news. What's up?"

"Ooooh." Maggie winced. "I thought you would have been the first. Can I back out now and start all over again?"

"I've got a little idea. Say it."

"Well, Ray, we got word this morning that Carol and Peter Kiel ran off and got married."

There was no response from Ray.

Will pursed his lips and picked coffee bubbles up in his spoon. "Where did they go?"

"To Indiana. They'll be back tomorrow — to his house by the river. It's not much of a honeymoon, but then —"

"But then," Ray finished with a downward inflection, "we should give you an award for surprises."

"Don't blame me," Maggie shrugged. "I only delivered the news. If I'd had my way, Carol would have been telling you that I had eloped."

*****

It was a week before Ray summoned enough nerve to pay Carol a visit. He went to Capitol City, took the drive by the river, and came at last to a fancy mailbox that proclaimed: PETER KIEL. The house was impressive, stone and wood, with gardens made private by a pebbly wall. Somehow he couldn't picture Carol in that setting. A ponytail and blue jeans wouldn't fit. But the Carol who answered his knock was not the girl but the woman he had seen often, with the cloak of dignity clutched tight about her. She invited him into a grand living room, making no attempt to explain herself.

Before Ray was settled, Chips was in his lap, purring deep and squinting his eyes. Ray was astonished to se the cat and when he asked about it, Carol answered, "I told you Peter likes him. He would never make me give him up."

"But how can he stand having an animal about that hates him?"

"Most people couldn't, but that's the difference with Peter. He doesn't need reassuring. Chips doesn't bother him, except as a challenge. One day he'll win him over, you watch and see."

Ray gave the cat an extra pat in an unspoken plea to go on being the discriminating cat he was.

They talked about inconsequential things over the first drink; but with the second one cold in his hand, Ray came bluntly to the point. "Are you happy?" he asked.

Carol was startled out of complacency. "Of course. Why shouldn't I be happy?"

"I didn't ask for reasons, just an answer," Ray said.

"The answer is yes. Peter is miraculous."

"And things are just as you thought they would be?"

She shifted in the chair, recrossed her legs. "I can't say that, but what bride can? Living with a man is entirely different from seeing him a few hours a day. There are things you expected and things you didn't expect. It can't be any other way. Peter takes a lot of understanding. He's different."

Ray wanted to laugh at that, but probed. "How so?"

"You've never gotten to know him, Ray. I guess even I am a little surprised by him. I feel a bit — inadequate. He's such a dominant person. Does that make any sense?"

Her expression said that she didn't feel she should go on, but the nervousness in her hands said that she had to tell someone.

"That's one thing you should never feel, Carol. If there was ever a woman who couldn't be inadequate, you're that woman."

"I used to think that, conceited or not. Dad made me think that way. I thought Peter was a lot like Dad — gentle and understanding — but —"

"But he isn't," Ray finished for her.

"No, he's not gentle. At least, not often." She cast her eyes downward, embarrassed; and Ray knew what she meant exactly.

"You wouldn't think one week could make any difference," she continued, softly. "Not just one week. But it has. I've rather lost my bearings. Sometimes I get the feeling that I'm going to drown in him." She swallowed the rest of her drink and stood up. "Would you like to see around the house?"

Ray followed her on a tour of inspection, a bit envious as she opened one door after another. He hadn't known that Kiel was so well situated. Beside the living room, there was a library, dining room, and kitchen downstairs; and a curving staircase led up to five beautiful bedrooms.

"You know, I rather miss the old house," Carol mused. "It was a lot poorer in some ways, yet warmer in important ones. But Peter needs this place, so we're selling the other one."

"I know." Ray thought his news might be welcome. "I'm buying. And since it's a perfect place for Will to work, he's going to be my star boarder."

"For some reason, that makes me feel good," Carol said, sighing. "I can visit you, can't I?"

"You've got to like cats before you can get through the door," Ray chuckled.

She caught his hand, serious for a moment. "You've been wonderful about this, Ray. No scolding, no recriminations. I'm grateful. It was something I couldn't help."

"It's done, that's all," he answered simply.

Ray had hoped to leave before Kiel returned, but the sound of a convertible hit the drive and a few minutes later Kiel came through the french doors which led to the garden. He was limping heavily. Carol went to him. He didn't look at her but at Ray and said, icily, "So, you finally came to satisfy your curiosity?"

"Peter!" Carol cried. "That's rude."

"Nonsense," he retorted, cutting her off. "Dr. Harper and I understand each other quite well, don't we, Dr. Harper?"

"Maybe not well enough," Ray answered. "This visit was strictly social. I should think you'd value your wife highly enough to understand that she has friends."

"Well said," Kiel replied and limped over to seat himself in an armchair. "The day they invent soft sidewalks will be the day for me. Get me a drink, will you, Carol?"

"This is the first chance I've had to congratulate you, Kiel," Ray said. "You've gotten yourself a fine wife."

"Thank you; and I'm aware of it." Kiel replied icily.

Then the two men sat in silence until Carol returned. When she did, Kiel looked up at her and asked: "What have you done with your day?"

She was strangely shy. "Nothing except try to keep busy. I can't seem to fill my time."

Kiel answered her matter-of-factly, "You'll have to find something to amuse yourself. I don't want you to go stale on me."

Ray clenched his teeth to keep from making some remark and Kiel asked, amused: "What's the matter, Dr. Harper? You look rather shocked."

"It's because I am rather shocked," Ray said bluntly. "You have a way of saying things that can do that."

"Carol understands," Kiel answered. "She's in good hands and she knows it, don't you, pet?" The affection was unnatural, but Carol reached across to grasp his hand. "She knows what I expect of her and what I can give her in return. The first few weeks of marriage are always the hardest."

"I suppose so," Ray said. "But I was under the impression that they were supposed to be happy ones."

He waited for a response, but none came. Kiel seemed to regard him in the same light as he regarded Chips — just a small annoyance to tolerate and wait out. Ray couldn't figure that. Peter Kiel was a wall, but a soft one. He could absorb everything thrown at him and smile back.

"You and Chips are a lot alike, Dr. Harper," Kiel said suddenly. "Both of you are stubborn and determined. But one day, you and I will come to know each other better. I promise."

Carol pressed her quiet voice into the tight silence. "Would you like to stay for dinner with us, Ray? I'm still a good cook."

Ray stood up too quickly. "Thanks, but not this time. I've got an exam to write. Will you walk me out?"

She came, her heels soundless on the thick carpets, and held the door wide. He paused, meaning to say something, but there was no expectancy on her face. She didn't want him to say anything. He left quickly, the uneasiness shadowing him.

CHAPTER NINE

Carol waited in the quiet house for the sound of the convertible or the ring of the doorbell. Both were infrequent. In one month of marriage, she had learned to putter. Because of Kiel's insistence, she was cut off from her friends, with no one to talk to but the housekeeper. And the housekeeper didn't like to talk. Carol had never been at loose ends before; but now it seemed that whenever Peter was absent, there wasn't a thing in the world to do.

She needed someone to help clear her mind — someone to listen and lead her back to the world of sense. Sometimes, talking to Peter, there was no world of sense. He said things that had no possible meaning; yet he said them with such authority that she knew it was her fault that she didn't understand. And if she let him know that she was lost, the look of frustrated pity that swept his face hurt her almost physically.

The muffled growl of tires on gravel sent Chips scurrying out of the room and Carol braced herself, deciding the time to talk was now. There wouldn't be a better one.

The door swung open and Peter limped inside, rubbing his hands. "I didn't expect it to turn so cold. There could at least have been some warning."

Carol stood motionless, only her fingers hinting at emotion. "I want to talk to you, Peter," she said softly.

"Good," he caught her by surprise. "I've been hoping you'd shake this apathy and be yourself." He limped to the davenport and stretched into a comfortable position, expectant. "What is it going to be? A complaint and demand session?"

"I didn't intent to put it that way. I just wanted to talk."

"Well? I'm waiting."

She didn't like the opening, but she took it anyway. "It's not a complaint," she said. "It's just that I feel left out of everything. I'm used to being active, you know that, and I can't sit in the background."

He didn't become angry, as she half expected, or dominant, as she thoroughly expected. Instead, he commented, "I thought your conception of a happily married woman was one who is pampered, provided for, and cherished."

"That idea went out years ago." She was amazed; her father might have said those words, but not Peter Kiel. "I can't explain it exactly, but I feel as though I'm fading away — as though my ideas, my thoughts — everything I should be able to call my own — are slipping from me."

"What do you suggest? I can't give you back those things."

"I didn't ask that." She caught his hand. "I've tried to work it out, and I think what I need most are contacts with my friends. I had quite a few friends, Peter. Now, all of a sudden, I'm cut off from them. You could give your consent to have Ray and Will here once in a while. I'd like to see them."

He pressed her hand in both of his gently. "I told you I would select your friends. You've got to have faith in me."

"I do have faith in you," she protested. "That's the simplest thing in the world. But I can't understand."

"We're going somewhere, Carol, and we have to be careful."

She pulled away before he could make her surrender. "I know what you're trying to say, but it doesn't make sense. There's no reason in the world to be careful of Ray."

Kiel's eyes grew hard. "Then, let's put it this way. *I* have to be careful of him. I know what's best."

"You mean because he doesn't like you?"

"What he thinks of me is of no concern," Kiel growled, out of patience with her doubts. "He's a middle-man, and I can't be bothered with middle-men right now."

Carol's mind struggled with the words. "I don't follow you, Peter. I don't know what you're talking about."

He rose to walk about. "I like to know where a man stands, Carol, where he fits. I have to know. If he's weak, all right — if he's strong, all right; then I have some ground to work on. But the ones in the middle exasperate me. If I challenge and they fall, then I've wasted time. But if I challenge and they don't fall, then I've bitten off more than I want right now. Ray Harper is in the middle, and I want no contact with him."

"What do you mean, challenge?"

"You don't understand," he answered gruffly. "You never will. Just forget about it and do as I say."

"But that's not fair!"

"You've picked the wrong time to oppose me, Carol. This hits too close. I've said all I'm going to say, and you'll have to accept it."

"I won't accept it!"

"That's where you're wrong," he answered, menace clear in his tone. "If you can't understand, I forgive you for it. I realize your limitations. But you are my wife and I expect you to fit into my life and my plan. It may be difficult, but I demand it."

A shiver raced through her. "No! I will not accept anything that is so unjust."

His black eyes were upon her. There was hunger in them, and purpose. She staggered backward, hands against her head, trying to contain the sudden pain that threatened to tear it apart. She swayed and he caught her as she began to sink to her knees.

"You must rest," he said quietly, all the anger gone. "You've upset yourself too much."

"Did you do that to me, Peter?" she whimpered.

He helped her to her feet. "I'll get you up to bed. You're cold."

"I'm not cold," she cried. "I don't know why I'm trembling. Where's Mr. Chips? I want him."

"We'll find him. Come along."

*****

There was a chill in the air made of dry wind and the promise of snow. Everything was barren with an unpleasant touch of nakedness. It made Ray's mood more urgent as he remembered Carol's queer phone call.

They swerved into Kiel's drive and Ray said, "She wants to come with us, Will. For some reason, she doesn't want to stay in the house." He turned off the motor, but didn't move to get out.

"What's wrong?" Will asked.

"I don't know. I guess I'm afraid to go to the door."

"For heaven's sake, get going," Will commanded. "Find out what it's all about."

Ray went quickly up the walk. Will watched from the car as Carol appeared, already wrapped in a blue coat. He got out of the car so that she could slide to the middle of the front seat.

Ray waited until they were well under way before he asked: "Where to, Carol?"

"To your house?" Her voice was almost inaudible. "If it's not too much bother."

"What do you mean, bother?" Ray sensed something strange in the girl beside him. Her presence was there; her body was warm where it touched his; and her face was the same. But the sameness ended there.

"I don't like to leave Chips alone too long. I'll have to get back soon," Carol said suddenly.

Ray took her elbow. "Look here, Mrs. Kiel, we've finally gotten you here and you're going to stay for a while, understand?"

When they had reached Ray's house and were settled in the living room, Ray opened some soft drinks; but they weren't much help as icebreakers. Carol remained huddled on the davenport with nothing to offer. Finally, Will took the situation into his own hands.

"What's wrong with you, Carol?"

"Wrong? I didn't know there was anything wrong with me."

Ray forced his voice to remain quiet as he asked: "What did you want to talk about? You sounded urgent on the phone."

Carol picked up her drink, running her hands along the wet sides of the glass. She waited so long to reply that the two men thought she wasn't going to answer at all. "I wanted your help — if you'll give it. There's something wrong with my husband."

The simple words hit at the men, but they waited for her to continue. "I suppose I'm just a jealous, suspicious wife; but I don't know what he does, you see; and I'd like to know." Her voice was almost a whimper. "He won't tell me where he goes or what he does. I thought maybe you could find out."

She looked from one to the other of them like a lost child. Ray felt his insides clench tight. "What happened to you, Carol?" He moved over beside her. "Has he mistreated you?"

"No!" she showed emotion for the first time. "He'd never do that. He tries. It's just that I can't understand. Sometimes I think he lives in another world — one where words mean different things and people do different things. But he tries."

Ray found his thoughts echoed across Will's face: this wasn't rational talk; this wasn't even Carol!

"I thought that if I knew where he goes and what he does," Carol went on, "maybe I could understand him better. He says strange things. Sometimes I think I'm losing my mind." She grabbed Ray's hands. "Am I going crazy? Tell me. Am I?"

"Do you want to see a doctor?" Ray asked calmly. "I'll take you to the Psych Clinic if you want to go."

"No." She turned from pleading to nervous determination. "I have to go home. Will you find out for me? What I asked?"

"Of course. But what about you?"

She put on her coat, oddly in a hurry. "I'll be all right once I find out. You just don't know — he's such a strong, strong man. I have to find something to hold on to; then maybe I won't drown."

Ray pulled her to face him. "Look, Carol, I'm going to take you to a doctor right now. I've heard enough of this."

"No! Please! Let me go home. If you don't take me — I'll walk. I have to hurry. Peter wants me home."

Ray gave in and took her to the car. She didn't offer another word all the way. Kiel's convertible was in the drive when they arrived and he came out on the steps to meet them, immediately taking possession of Carol, circling her in one arm.

"She's not feeling well, Kiel," Ray said carefully, holding back the rush of angry words that wanted to burst out.

"I know. She shouldn't have gone out at all. If I had been here, she wouldn't have. Thanks for bringing her home and don't worry about her, Dr. Harper. I'm quite capable of taking care of my wife."

He turned and took Carol inside without a good-by.

CHAPTER TEN

The process of investigating Peter Kiel began. Will and Ray started with from nothing. The man existed, they knew that, and that was all. What he did, or what he planned to do, was unknown. A politician doesn't go through life unknown; he leaves a trail behind him — a trail of people, because people are his life blood.

The logical place to begin was at either of the two party headquarters. The first office was drab, without the flood of bright posters that come with election year.

Yes, they knew Peter Kiel, and wasn't he a wonderful man? No, he wasn't affiliated formally with their party; but didn't they wish he were? He would be the next governor no matter who ran against him. No, they didn't really know anything about his background except that he was well versed in political theory, according to the powers who were concerned with such things. A man with his forceful personality could go as far as he wanted.

Will thanked them, ducked their return questions, and walked the few blocks to the twin; but opposite, party office. "Twin" was the correct word, for the answers were the same: "Not affiliated yet. Wonderful man. No known background."

Will decided to see some of the state legislators. Any good bar close to the capitol building should yield a small covey of them. But to his surprise, the larger percentage of the men didn't know Peter Kiel. The few who did shook their heads seriously, muttering, "Good man, good man. A man to watch."

Only one had any adverse words. He stated bluntly: "I don't much like the man, but I've got to admire him just the same. He hits you full force the first time you meet him, and you never forget. There's something compelling about him — magnetic. He's making a point of mingling with people, important people. Come back next week, and I doubt if you'll find one man here who doesn't know him."

The personal opinions were of little surprise. Will had heard them once before, expressed in more dramatic terms by a French exchange student. The boy had met Kiel, and his description of that meeting had never left Will's mind. The boy had turned up at Ray's office to ask for Kiel's address.

"I want to find that man again," he said. "I have to meet him again."

When Will asked why, he answered melodramatically: "Because when I met him for the first time, it was like a splash of cold water in my face. I think I died a little then. He took something from me and I want to get it back."

Will realized that, in a way, he himself was like the boy, searching for something that didn't exist. And Ray was forced to agree with him, although he was determined not to give up on Carol. There was just one conclusion to be drawn from the things Ray had seen. Either there was something vitally wrong with Kiel or there was something vitally wrong with Carol. It wasn't pleasant to think about the latter, but it had to be considered.

Ray decided to have a talk with one of the staff members of the psychiatric clinic. One who had met Kiel. If it wasn't Carol who was insane, it had to be Kiel.

*****

Three nights in a row, men had come to the house. They came in, unwrapped themselves from expensive coats, and disappeared into the living room with Peter. Carol was never introduced to them, for Peter ordered her to remain upstairs. She knew the reason. He was ashamed. On the third night, she forced herself to remain calm about it, lying on her big bed, petting Mr. Chips.

Chips had a magic quality. He could bring her peace. He had always been able to calm her with his special combination of silken warmth and hypnotic purr. But now, he had come to be more than that. She felt better when she was with the cat — a little more herself, a little less confused.

Mr. Chips wasn't as gay as he had been in the old house. Now he played with her through the day, but his evenings were spent watching.

"I guess I've joined you, Tiger," Carol said to him that night. "I'm watching, too."

Then, suddenly, she stood up, tying her robe tight. "Maybe neither of us will have to wait any longer," she said to the cat. "I'm going down to meet our guests. I don't know what's come over me; but Peter will be angry, so you stay here."

The men were in the living room, two strangers and Peter, their voices jovial. Taking a long breath, Carol stepped into the light. "Good evening, gentlemen. I thought I'd just peek in for a moment."

Peter was beside her in four wide steps, his hand hard on her arm. The two men rose politely, their attitudes showing concern; and Carol wondered what Peter had told them. Kiel introduced her, his eyes roaming to the men with a silent message.

The short one, called Pearson, took Carol's hand. "I'm very

glad to have met you, my dear; and I hope you'll be feeling better soon." He glanced at Peter. "You have a lovely wife, Kiel."

"She is," Kiel said flatly. "She'll excuse you if you have to go."

Pearson cleared his throat awkwardly. "I'll get in touch with you tomorrow."

Peter showed the men to the door and Carol sat down stiffly. When Peter's halting step returned, she looked away.

"What did you think you were doing?" he demanded. "Did you deliberately want to embarrass me?"

"Why should I embarrass you?"

"I told those men that you were ill — in bed. Then you walk in here. You may just as well have said, 'My husband lied; I'm not ill at all.'"

"I'm not," she said.

"Sometimes I wonder about that." His tone was low with disgust. "Look at you, cowering in that chair like a beaten animal. Why do you think I ask you to stay out of the way when I have guests?"

"I don't know, Peter," she whispered.

"Because you're so much of a jellyfish. I want a wife — a woman — not a cringing, whimpering 'creature'!"

She faced him for the first time. "That's half the reason I came down; I wanted to show you that I'm not a jellyfish."

"The coming down, I wouldn't have minded. That wasn't the crime. The crime was the look on your face. You should have seen yourself. You looked like a lost child, frightened" — he whirled away from her — "I shouldn't have married you at all."

"No, you can't say that!" she cried, and threw her arms around him. But he wouldn't yield. "I've tried — everything I know. It seems to me that *you're* not trying." Her voice broke.

"Stop it! Do you hear? Why can't you be yourself? What makes you wilt every time you talk to me?"

"Please," she trembled, visibly attempting to take control of herself. "I don't understand it either. I try; but you're smothering me, that's what you're doing — all of my thoughts, all of my confidence — it's all smothered. If only you'd have a little patience and a little compassion. You're too strong for me. You don't realize it, but you're like some horrible overpowering force that I can't fight. You must have a little compassion, a little giving in you somewhere."

"That's not the way the world is. You can't be soft or you'll lose yourself."

"How can you lose yourself?" she demanded.

"It's a simple matter of control or be controlled — assert yourself or be taken by someone else. There are the strong and the weak. The weak are nothing and I won't be one of them."

"Where did you get this idea? It's not true."

"It is true! That's the way life is!" Kiel's face was red with emotion — with a frustration that burned from the inside out. "And there's nothing you can do about it except to be strong and see that you come out on top. I've seen what happens when you let down. From childhood little children must fight for their identity or lose it completely. I came too close once, and I swore it would never happen to me."

"Fight for existence against what?"

"Against other people. You've seen it, Carol. Everyone I meet is measuring, maneuvering, trying to see if they will dominate or if I will dominate. I don't give them a chance. I take them first. The more I have, the safer I am, because the stronger I am. I can protect you."

"You're not protecting me, Peter. No matter what you think, you're hurting me."

"I know that," he answered, throwing down his hands, "and it doesn't have to be that way. If you'd do as I say for a while, until I'm secure — Look, Carol, I don't want to fight you. I *don't!* But you've forced me. You want to be better. Just leave me alone, leave my business alone; and you *can* be better. I promise."

"Your business!" Carol moved away. "I didn't even know what your business was until a week ago — and, in truth, I still don't. If Will couldn't figure it out, neither can I."

"Will? What does he have to do with this?"

"I didn't mean to tell you," she said, sighing.

"Obviously. But perhaps you'd better."

"I have no reason to be ashamed. I had Ray and Will do some checking for me. I wanted to find out where you go and what you do. A wife should know those things."

When she looked at him, she stepped backward in alarm. His features twisted in bitter, seething anger. Then, suddenly, his expression changed and he clasped his hands, then smiled. "You've just managed to get your two friends back, Carol," he said. "You've done the only thing that would make me let them in this house. Now they *must* come. Invite them to dinner if you like. Anything. I'm ready now. It's sooner than I wished, but I'm ready."

His tone made Carol realize that the fury she had seen in him moments before hadn't vanished. She suddenly wanted to run upstairs and find Chips.

"You've done your last bit of prying behind my back, however," he advanced. "I can't have any more of it. I've asked you, I've pleaded with you, and you won't listen. I have no choice."

CHAPTER ELEVEN

Doctor McGregor was a short, broad man with a tint of sand in his hair and a line of red at his upper lip. His eyes were blue with a keenness that was out of place with his baggy tweeds.

"When the girl gave me your note, Ray," he said, "I was quite amazed. But the more I thought about it, the more interesting it became."

"I realize it's an odd request, and probably a difficult one," Ray answered.

"I've only met Peter Kiel twice, and there's really nothing one can say about a person after two meetings."

"An ordinary person, I agree," Ray commented. "But Kiel affects people. He must have affected you."

The wry smile curled around the pipe stem protruding from McGregor's mouth. "He did."

"Normally, I wouldn't ask this of anyone, but you've had a lot of experience, Mac. You probably know as much about him as anyone does, just from hearsay."

"Here, and in town," said McGregor, nodding, "I have some friends in the senate and they're convinced that he's up to something. The odd thing is, they don't care."

"What is your opinion? Point blank — is he crazy?"

"That's a big word. I'll give you a big answer. Yes and no."

"You win," Ray chuckled. "I won't hurry you again."

"No, I meant that," McGregor assured him. "There are certain people who lie outside our set rules of psychosis and neurosis. We've labeled them, but we don't really understand them. 'Pathological personality' is the general label, and under that, 'antisocial personality.' They're usually above average in intelligence and quite charming, at first glance. But they are completely unable to understand or accept ethical values or restraint. To the best of our knowledge, they have no conscience."

"You mean they have no standards of right and wrong?"

"Exactly. They do a thing because they want to do it. They can lie and feel nothing. They can kill and feel no remorse. They're a race unto themselves and we don't know how they got that way. They don't respond well to treatment."

"And you think Kiel is one?"

"I think so, from what I've heard of his lack of compassion and guilt."

"Then he could be dangerous," Ray concluded, sitting forward.

"Very dangerous. He has one of those rare magnetic personalities and could be a great man. But he misuses his power and that's why he's doubly dangerous. Don't you see? He can draw people to him and then he has no conscience to govern his actions toward them." He tapped his pipe clean and immediately refilled it. "If I were you, Ray, I wouldn't press him too hard. Don't arouse him."

"He's changed his tune. I got a call from Carol this morning and Will and I are invited out there for dinner tomorrow night. *His* invitation."

"Don't be fooled. Whatever he does is strictly for his own benefit. If he has invited you, it's for a reason."

"And I want to go for a reason." Ray's forehead creased. "Peter Kiel or no Peter Kiel. I have to help Carol. Is it possible for a girl like Carol to go off the deep end?"

"Carol's the last person in the world I'd expect to do that," Mac stated. "Her father's death was a shock, yes, but she's always been perfectly adjusted. She'd roll with it."

"That's what I thought, and yet she's changed. I wanted to bring her over here the other day, but she wouldn't come. She won't do anything without his express permission. So I did the only thing I could think of to do."

"What's that?"

"Carol asked me to bring along an extra guest, a woman, so she wouldn't feel outnumbered. It dawned on me that maybe I could take advantage of the invitation and I invited Jenny Peck."

"Jenny Peck? What do you want with a telepath?"

"Don't laugh, Mac. Jenny can read thoughts. I remember Grayson telling me he had a plan to use her as a sounding board for psychotics. He thought that telepaths could be used to advantage that way — where the psychologist can only watch and guess, the telepath can go into the psychotic's mind."

"I know all about that," Mac admitted reluctantly. "It's a closely kept secret, but Grayson and I attempted it once or twice."

"You did? Then I wasn't so far off. I thought Jenny could do the same thing for Carol. If I just knew what was bothering Carol, I'd have a place to start."

"Does Carol know Jenny?"

"Not very well. Anyway I've got an excuse, if I need one. Kiel's interested in telepathy, and I can say I brought Jenny along for some parlor-type experiments."

*****

Jenny was a quiet little woman, with big brown eyes and shiny hair.

To one who didn't know her, she was mousy and uninteresting. To one who knew her, she was listening.

She had listened to Ray's explanation intently and didn't like the secrecy of the plot. But she had accepted for Carol's sake.

The Kiel house had sprouted a maid and cook. Kiel was doing the evening up in grand style. As Carol stood beside him to welcome them, she seemed to be her own self, confident and easy; yet there was a nervousness in her hands.

Kiel went out of his way to be polite and even disarming, showing them the charm that had won him so many friends. Jenny was immediately captivated, her face flushed pink, her movements and speech quickened.

Carol looked better than she had in weeks, and Ray said so. He had to admit that Kiel provided for her in good fashion. But when they moved to the dining room and Carol's chiffon stole swayed from her upper arm, he saw a wide bruise, blue and purple against her skin.

The talk at dinner was more chatter than conversation. Kiel continued in his role as host with Jenny hanging on to every word he said.

They dawdled over a surprising winter dessert of fresh strawberries; then roamed back to the big living room for coffee. Ray commented on the conspicuous absence of his tiger-cat friend.

"He's upstairs," Kiel explained. "I thought I'd like to be free from those staring eyes for one evening."

"You haven't made any more progress with him?"

"No. The cat is just naturally antisocial with me."

Ray caught a movement from Will out of the corner of his eye and followed his lead to Jenny. The girl's eyes were alive, fastened on Kiel as though she might devour him. "Then if you haven't won Chips, you haven't gone much further on your theories of animal telepathy. Did they bog down somewhere?"

Jenny straightened as Kiel answered. "I don't take back any of my statements, if that's what you mean. What I said was true — I just haven't the time I need to —"

Suddenly Kiel's head jerked up and his face tightened. He slammed his coffee cup on the table and sprang to his feet with reflex action. His eyes combed the room, coming to rest on Jenny, where they stared in an alertness that was part fright and part antagonism. Before Ray could gasp out a question, Jenny gathered up her long skirt and ran for the hall. As she brushed by, Ray saw that one hand was to her mouth and her cheeks were pale. She looked suddenly and deathly sick.

"What's the matter?" Carol cried.

"That's what I'd like to know," Kiel growled. "Maybe you should go after her, Carol. She looked ill."

Carol left in a flurry of chiffon, calling the maid to help. Ray was on his feet, bewildered. He knew that Jenny wasn't sick in any normal way.

Kiel said coolly: "I told Carol that cook was no good. I hope the girl doesn't hold it against us." His voice was definite, a cynical look of understanding coupled with it.

"We should probably take her home," Will said anxiously.

"Anything you say," Kiel agreed. "But finish your coffee. She'll be awhile." He returned to his chair and added hot coffee to his cup, the moment of startled confusion gone.

Ray shook his head, coming back to the glimpse he'd had of Jenny's face. "Don't worry about it, Dr. Harper," Kiel said, catching his expression. "Women are notoriously delicate. These things can come on quite suddenly."

"I suppose so," Ray admitted, "but I don't understand it. What made you jump up?"

"I saw her face — I knew she was sick."

"Jenny wants to go home, Ray," Carol interrupted from the door. "She'll be down in just a minute. She's awfully shaky. I think she should have a doctor, but she wouldn't let me call one."

"We'll take care of her," Will assured Carol.

"I'm sorry the evening has to end so soon," Kiel said, smiling. "But you'll come back again." It wasn't an invitation; it was a dare. And it caught Ray short.

Jenny appeared at the head of the stairs, pale and unsteady. Ray started for her, but Kiel moved faster and went halfway to meet her. Her arm stiffened where he touched her to help her down. Ray gathered Jenny in and hurried her out into the air. When the door closed behind them, she let out an audible sigh and ran for the car.

Ray started the engine and sped around the circular drive to the road. "What happened to you?"

"He knew," Jenny whispered. "He knew."

Will took hold of her hands, clasping them tight to stop the trembling. "What are you talking about, Jenny?"

Her voice rose to an unnatural pitch. "I had only found him when he jumped up. He knew, I tell you. I shouldn't have done it — but I only wanted to be nearer to him."

Ray understood then, in one quick flash of insight. "Did you try to read Peter Kiel's mind?" he gasped.

"I liked him; I wanted to know what went on behind those sharp eyes of his. If only I hadn't tried."

"Of all the —"Ray began.

"Don't scold," Jenny pleaded. "I paid for it. He knew what I was doing."

"Do you mean he's a telepath too?" Ray demanded.

"I don't know; he just sensed me, that's all. I touched his mind and he felt it."

"And that's when you got sick? Why did you get sick?"

"I can't explain it," she whispered. "You'd have to experience it to understand. I didn't get anything from him, but there was something there, and that's what made me sick."

"What you saw in his mind?"

"Yes. It was strange and violent. I couldn't make any sense out of it, but I felt it. When I first found him, he was calm, I knew that much; but it was still different from any mind I've seen before. All different. Then, suddenly it knotted — violent. That's when he jumped up, when he sensed me. He was frightened for a moment, and then — I can't describe it for you; but he crouched — mentally, he crouched, ready to pounce. Then that changed and I was frightened. I felt like I was going to fall over the edge of some bottomless pit, and the violence and tension in his mind turned my stomach over." She pulled her hands from Will's and clutched her stomach. "I wish Professor Grayson were here. Maybe he would know what I saw."

"Forget about it," Ray said. "You shouldn't have tried it in the first place."

"I never will again!" She was vehement. "He came up those stairs for me deliberately, do you know that? I think he enjoyed it. He knew I was afraid of him and revolted by him. I only worry for Carol. There's something wrong with her, Ray. It's him! You can't let her stay with him."

"There's nothing anyone can do about it. I realized that when I saw her tonight. She's made the adjustment, whatever it is, and now she belongs to him."

CHAPTER TWELVE

The month changed to December. Christmas stars, wreaths, and Santa Clauses appeared and snow fell in sparkling bits on the ground. Ray didn't hear from Carol often, and a stranger had to tell him that she and Kiel had gone away for two weeks.

Ray was tied up in his work one morning, checking the mimeographed sheets on his last exam, when Will, clutching an envelope, burst into his little office.

"Here it is," Will proclaimed. "Maybe it's the jackpot!"

He waited in controlled agitation as Ray opened the envelope. It contained a letter and a newspaper clipping — a short obituary. The principals were of Elisa and Joshua Betts. It simply said that they had been found dead in their mountain home by their son Luke. It gave the location as a post office in some obscure town called The Corners, and the cause of death was murder.

"That was in the *Carrolton News* way back in spring," Will explained. "Earl Logan, one of my friends was down there, dug it up for me after I asked him to keep his eyes open for something in Arkansas. It seems there was quite a commotion about it in the hills, but no solution."

"I don't get it," Ray puzzled.

"Earl made some inquiries. These people were found murdered all right — their heads were bashed in!"

"Oh!" Ray grunted. "Two more of them."

"Two more, and all ours for now. This story didn't reach the news wires, so we can investigate first."

"I take it you intend to go down?" Ray asked.

"Not alone. I want you with me."

*****

The town wasn't really a town at all, living up to its name of The Corners. It had one general store and three weather-beaten houses. Will and Ray wangled a guide, in the person of a small boy, to lead them to Luke Betts's house and resigned themselves to the long hike up the mountain.

As the sun stood high, they came in sight of the cabin. The boy pointed it out, took his money, and left them to go up alone.

"Boy," Will whistled, "what a place. Could anyone really enjoy living here?"

Ray smiled. "Be it ever so humble —"

They crossed a clearing where the wind blew cold, and they pounded on a rough-hewn door. It opened a crack and a woman's face peered at them. It was a smooth face, and clean, touching on prettiness.

"Are you Mrs. Luke Betts?" Will asked.

"Yup," came the reply.

"We'd like to talk to you. It's about your people."

"What people?" Her voice was cold.

"Elisa and Joshua Betts. Could we come in?"

The door drew wide and the whole woman appeared, a bit ungainly in old-fashioned clothes. "I figure it's near time somebody come to talk about thet."

They followed her into the warmth of the cabin, adjusting their eyes to the dim light. Another figure rose from before the fire — a tall man with a messy shock of black hair and a jutting face. "This here's my husband, Luke," the woman said. "I'm Min Betts."

Luke thrust his hand forward. "Glad to meet you." He didn't offer them chairs because there weren't enough to go around.

"Where you folks from?" Min asked.

"We're from Michigan."

"And you come all thet way to talk about Luke's folks?"

"We'd like to ask you some questions, if you don't mind."

"Thet's all right. I'll tell you anythin' you want to know."

Will asked for her version of the whole murder story.

She led them to a window and pointed down the mountain to a place where a chimney poked through the trees.

"Thet's where they lived. And thet's where they was found. Luke found 'em — their heads split wide open. The first we'd know'd anythin' was wrong was when their dog there" — she pointed to a limp bunch of spotted hair in the corner — "come up and wouldn't go home. Luke went down and he found 'em. They're buried down there in the clearin'."

"Do you have any idea how it happened?"

"They had a man stayin' with 'em. Luke went close by there one day and saw him out with Joshua. We figured he's the one who done it."

"Then you saw him?" Will asked Luke.

"Jist from a distance," he answered. "I saw Josha helpin' him around a bit and heard him talkin'. The man was hurt, I know'd that. He couldn't walk by hisself."

"Can you remember how he looked?"

"He was tall as me, and broader — more filled out. He had black hair and, like I say, he couldn't walk. Josha called him Ezekiel — I heard that. But the man, he didn't answer."

Ray clapped Will on the shoulder.

"Thet was the same day the big wind come from across the hill," Min threw in. "Near blew the roof off the cabin."

"Did blow up all the trees over there," Luke added. "When I went over, there wasn't nothin' all around. A strange thing. You'd a thought somebody'd made a spell, the way it was."

"Could you tell what was wrong with the man? Why he couldn't walk?"

"One of his legs was no good, I guess," Luke replied. "I think it to be his left one." He closed his eyes visualizing it. "Yup, his left one. One of his hands was wrapped up too. But thet's all I kin tell you. We don't know nothin' else."

"Do you have any idea where the man went?"

"We think he didn't go nowhere. He didn't come from no-where earthly, so he couldn't go back to nowhere, could he? Thet dog over there, now he could tell you plenty. He seen it all, from thet first light thet dropped down, to the end. He could tell you."

"Light?"

"It fell out of the sky, right over there where Luke seen the place with all the trees blown away. The dog begun his howlin' thet night."

"You're talking about a meteor," Ray half stated.

"It jist was a thing, all lit up purple. We seen it come down. We was scared to go over; but Luke finally went, after Li and Josha was found. There weren't nothin' there. No grass, no trees, nothin'. You want Luke to show you the place? It's still bare. It never growed up agin last summer."

"Would you take us over?" Will asked.

"Wait till I git my coat. It's a goodly walk."

They walked downhill, the spotted dog in their wake. Finally they broke into a clearing and the counterpart of Luke's cabin squatted before them. The dog stopped short of the cleared space.

"He don't never come close to thet cabin since it happened," Luke drawled. "I guess he remembers."

They entered the dirty place, sweeping cobwebs and dust aside, the smell of disuse coming up strong and musty. It was bare and uninteresting except for some stains on the floor. "Ma was lyin' there," he pointed. "It was worse than anythin' I ever seen durin' the war."

"You've been outside here then?" Will asked. "I mean, you've seen something beside these mountains?"

"I seen enough to know thet wasn't no fallin' star thet come down across the hill. Min thought it was, but I know'd better."

"And you believe it was something supernatural," Ray stated, trying to job Will back to normalcy. "A hex light, maybe?"

"No, I don't." Luke's face was firm and his eyes level. "I think it was one of them flyin' saucers."

Ray dropped his hands in a gesture of "What next?" It was Will's show now. But Will was busily poking about the cabin.

Soon they started out again, the dog returning to their company. It wasn't much farther before they came upon another clearing. But this one wasn't like the others. This was too barren, too sterile. There wasn't a standing tree in a radius of a hundred feet, and not a stone lying on the hard-packed ground. The trees along the exact edge of the circle were discolored on one side, and the limbs that had reached out over the cleared space were gone, sliced off neatly.

Will didn't offer a word. Neither did Ray. This was a bit more than he had expected. Luke stood on his skinny legs like a frozen crane, awe written in every line. He was anxious to get away from the place and hurried them back to their own trail, shook hands around, and left.

Ray asked, a weak smile on his face, "Well, now that you've seen it, what do you think? Or are you convinced that it was a flying saucer?"

"I don't know," Will muttered, "but I'm going to investigate."

"You're not serious?"

Will reached in his pocket. "Maybe this will help your scientific mind." He handed Ray a small object. It was a button, metal and silver colored. Ray squinted at the pattern pressed into it, but couldn't make it out. "I found that in the cabin," Will explained, his tone almost triumphant. "I can't decipher it. I can't even recognize the pictured symbols. If you can, then you've got the answer to our question right now."

He drew something else from his pocket. "You went into the cabin with your mind negatively set and you came out empty-handed. I went in looking for something and I found it. There was a pile of clothes and junk under the bed. I found the button there and I found this."

He gave Ray a circular piece of cloth, bright-colored and printed in the same foreign symbols. The only thing it could be compared with was an army sleeve patch designating a particular outfit. An oblong purple thing was set against a background of silver stars.

"This might have come out of a cereal box for kids."

"And the writing?" Will left the tone open.

"I don't know. But a language specialist would be able to tell you, if it's not just gibberish to mystify children."

*****

The story broke in the Carrolton papers the day they gave it to the police. In the spring it had warranted only a paragraph; now it loomed to headlines all across the nation.

From Carrolton Will contacted the papers in every town within a forty-mile radius of the mountain where the light had fallen; and he placed a want ad in their columns, asking for information. It was a strange ad, and its success hinged on having the right persons read it and understand.

Two days passed with no results. But on Wednesday the hotel phone rang and Will listened to a frightened voice announce itself as Mr. Ed Moore who said he had to talk to someone before he lost his mind. He gave an address, and Will picked up Ray and drove to the residential section of town.

Ed Moore gave the impression of a man who hadn't slept in weeks. Harried and pale, he paced in front of his two visitors. "I can't shake the feeling that this may be my fault. I was a coward, and people may be dead because of it. I saw the light you're after. I can give you a complete description of it."

Will pulled out his pencil and copied the words — purple, glowing, tremendous speed, no sound. Moore tried to explain the terrible emotions he had known when he saw the thing. His wife came in to corroborate that part of it.

Will tried to feel vicariously the things Moore had described, but such fear was impossible to imagine. He glanced to Moore's bookshelves and noticed a long row of books dealing with flying saucers. "I see you've studied up on the saucers."

"I didn't have one of those books when it happened!" Moore answered emphatically. "I started studying them after I saw the thing. I wasn't predisposed to seeing it."

Will conceded the point with relief. Ray would have jumped on it if he hadn't cleared it away.

"Anyway," Moore continued, "to the best of my knowledge, this wasn't a flying saucer. It was a machine — an alien machine. Saucers are one breed of cat; this was another. The only one of its kind, as far as I can see from the reports. I hope to God that's true."

The man looked sick, as though something inside was going to gnaw through at any moment. "When I read about the murders, I didn't think any more of it than anyone else did. But — that Betts family that was right across from where I saw the machine fall. Maybe if I had reported what I saw, whatever it is that is running around loose would have been stopped before it had a chance to get started." He turned to them, pleading for assurance. "Could that be? Am I responsible?"

"No," Will said. "A *man* committed those murders — a man who has been seen. It wasn't any monster."

"Is this true?" Moore's face said he wanted to believe it more than he wanted anything else in the world.

"It's true." Ray added his conviction to Will's.

The man wilted, changing from a prowling bunch of nerves to a tired lump of relief.

Back in the car, Will asked: "Do we take his word, or don't we?"

"I'm with you," Ray muttered. "It was something out of the sky, and the man Josha Betts was helping to walk was injured in the crash. His name is Ezekiel and we've got to find him."

*****

The next stop on their trip to the northeast was southern Indiana. Ray and Will searched for someone who had known the Babcocks well enough to supply information and came up with Joe Benson. He was a lonely old man whose sole companion was a cat named Boots who stuck to him like a furry ball.

Benson told them about Ezekiel. He'd hired a man by that name and description to work his acre and had intended to send him to the Babcocks. But he couldn't agree on the accent. He was positive it was Tennessee, not Arkansas, and swore he'd know the difference. When they questioned him about the last name, he couldn't help. The man had only said his name was Ezekiel — from the Bible.

Their other stops were fruitless. They couldn't uncover anyone else who had seen their man and lived to tell about it.

CHAPTER THIRTEEN

A nine-foot tree stood in the living room, dripping silver and gold trimming, and hovering over a brood of presents. Carol was ensconced on the davenport. Her welcome wasn't warm; it just wasn't anything. She held out her hand to Ray and it was lifeless. Chips luxuriated beside her, sleek and shiny-furred. Carol's hand was constantly on him somewhere, smoothing his coat or clutching his tail.

Ray took the proffered seat uncomfortably. It wasn't pleasant to make conversation with a shell. To the question, "What have you been doing lately?" Carol answered haltingly:

"We went to a party last night. All of the big people. Plush." Her face closed in on itself and her eyes glazed. "Only they turned out not to be big people after all. They were all midgets beside Peter. He grew and grew and they shrank away."

Will cleared his throat and changed the topic. "It looks like you've bought out the town."

"No, those all came here. From friends."

The subject was closed. There could be no conversation when every question was answered with a flat statement.

"Look, Carol, there's something on your mind," Ray said bluntly. "What is it?"

She took on a look of sadness. "I can't get that poor girl out of my mind. I thought she was so nice."

"Who is that?"

"Jenny Peck. The Jenny you brought here. It's in the morning paper. At least she was happy when she died."

Will sprang to his feet. "Where's the paper?"

The story was on the front page with a picture of Jenny. Another picture showed her body being carried down a snowy hill. Found twelve feet from the ski trail in a little gully, she had been dead for six days, from skull fracture. There were no clues.

Ray was sick and made a round of strong drinks to fight it down. But Will picked up the phone and called Detroit. When he hung up, he was puzzled. "Her head was banged up the usual way, so it looks like our killer. Only — remember what I told you about the brains? Hers wasn't! It was normal."

"Then it might not have been murder," Ray said.

"They say it was. They found the place where the body originally fell. There was blood all over, but nothing that could have done that to her head. She was carried from that spot and dumped in the gully. Maybe we should go and have a look around."

"He wouldn't be there now; he never lingers. Did you stop to wonder — why Jenny? Why two murders so close to us? Grayson and a woman connected with him?"

Footsteps on the stairs turned them around. Kiel came down, taking the steps slowly, favoring his lame leg. He was dressed casually and there was a pleasant smile on his face, but it didn't quite reach his eyes. "I didn't know you were here," he said. "Carol should have called me."

Carol had Chips on her lap, but the cat's attention was immediately focused on Kiel.

"We stopped by to deliver some presents," Ray explained.

Kiel noticed the paper in Ray's hand. "That was a shock, wasn't it? Your directional theory proved to be right. It's too bad. She seemed such a harmless little thing."

The mention of Jenny coming from Kiel brought Ray's thoughts around in a sharp curve to the night of the dinner and what Jenny had said afterwards. She had been afraid of Kiel.

"I understand you two were responsible for uncovering those murders in Arkansas," Kiel said. "What could anyone have wanted with two people like that?"

"That's a good question," Will mused. "You said once that we should look for our motive in something taken from the victims. They had nothing worth taking."

"Then your lunatic answer must be right," Kiel commented, brushing aside further conjecture. "Anyway, going northeast, he's probably moved into Canada." He stood up. "This isn't any kind of talk for the Christmas season. Would you gentlemen like a drink?"

"Of course they would," Carol said. She was oddly brighter now that Kiel had joined them. There was more there when Ray looked at her; the shell had refilled itself.

As he poured the drinks, Kiel asked: "Did you discover anything else of importance in the South?"

"As a matter of fact, we did," Ray told him. "We saw Luke and Min Betts, the old couple's relatives. They said they saw the man who killed their folks."

"Oh? You have a description then?"

"A very good one. Right down to the basic details." As Kiel's hand stretched out to give Ray a glass, Ray's eyes focused on the scar that traveled in a red line up Kiel's wrist to back of his arm. Ray's breath caught sharply, and Kiel immediately pulled his sweater sleeve down to cover the mark.

"What does he look like?" Carol's tone was excited.

Kiel's eyes flashed at her, then away.

"He's tall," Ray told her, his voice deliberately insinuating. "He has black hair and a good body — except for a bad left leg, a limp. And maybe an injured arm."

Kiel's hand tightened on the glass and he grew wary.

But Will added, "And he has a strong southern drawl."

Ray was angry because Will had made him remember that fact.

"He sounds charming," Carol laughed, her fingers stroking the cat too hard. Chips didn't stand for it and moved off her lap.

"That animal," Kiel growled. "I'm going to buy him a blindfold. He just plain hates me and the feeling is becoming mutual. He gives it off like a generator."

Ray glanced at his watch, strangely on edge. "We've got to get along." He stood. "It's been good to see you both again. Let's get together more often."

"Yes, I think we should," Kiel said, surprising Ray with his friendliness. "It's time we got to know each other better." He walked them to the door. His closeness bothered Ray: so near, the man radiated something electric.

The car doors were barely shut when Will jumped down Ray's throat. "What did you think you were doing in there? Kiel was trying to be sociable and you gave him a pointed description of himself as the murderer. I've never heard a more open insult."

"Then you saw it, too?"

"What?"

"That the description fit."

"Physically, yes, but what about the accent?"

"Look, Will, I was just going on a sudden hunch, something I couldn't ignore. I was sitting there and things crystallized."

"Are you serious?"

"I don't know. But did you see the effect it had on him? For the first time *he* was in the corner."

"What can you expect when a man's confronted with the things you said? You're reading things into this that aren't there."

"Could be. But think about this. When you remove the first three letters from Ezekiel, what do you have left?"

*****

Two days later, on Will's stubborn insistence, Ray called Carol and asked to see her. She refused at first, but he wore her down. She submitted to any suggestion made in a firm enough voice.

When they picked her up, she appeared with a curious bundle

of brown fur shut up in a fancy carrying case. The bundle grunted at Ray. It was Chips.

"What are you doing with him?" Ray asked.

"I want him with me," Carol said. "He goes or I don't. And if we're going to talk, I want to get as far away from the house as I can. I have to." She clutched his arm. "Ray, I'm beginning to understand and I'm frightened. I need you."

He took the basket and carried Chips to the car. Will moved over, but Carol insisted on riding in back with the cat. She pointed the way to a public park some three miles from town, deserted because of winter; and Ray drew up beside the one closed building that stood on the grounds.

"What did you want to see me about?" Carol asked.

"It was Will's doing," Ray explained. "I put some ideas in his head and he insists on following them as truth."

Carol opened Chips's basket and let him roam about the car and on the ledge of the rear window. "I suppose it's about Peter. I heard what you were saying the other day — the broad hints. Peter was upset about it for a while. Maybe if you ask questions, I can give some answers."

"Just maybe?"

"I only mean that I don't think I can volunteer anything. I don't even know if I can talk about it. Peter wouldn't like me to be here." She reached for Chips and gathered him close. His purr was audible through the car. "I think this is the only friend I have in the world. I feel safe with him." She drew a deep breath and blurted: "Ray, is it possible for a person to lose her intelligence? To regress mentally?"

Ray moved on the seat to half face the back of the car. "Why ask a question like that?"

"Because I think I'm doing it. Right now I'm all right; I know what you're saying. But soon you'll say something and I won't be able to follow you. Peter does it all the time. He says such strange things and I don't know what he means." She was afraid to let them interrupt for fear she couldn't start again. "There's deep violence in him, and brutality. He feels that he has to master everyone or something terrible will happen to him. I'm frightened of him. He's wild inside."

Ray told her about his conversation with Doctor McGregor.

"That's not all true," she protested. "It makes sense, but it isn't Peter." She clutched Chips and lowered her voice as though imparting some dreadful secret that should never be spoken aloud. "I think Peter is a telepath. He can do weird things. I've seen him turn people to his own way. It's hard to explain because it's a fight to talk about it at all. I feel that he's watching me even now. But he has a hold over people, Ray, and he grows stronger all the time. I've seen him come home from parties where he's met many people and he's exhilarated. He looks taller, stronger, as though he's taken some new life from those people."

Ray drew out his cigarettes and passed the pack around.

Chips had curled up in the back window, deciding to make the best of a confusing situation and view the birds that flashed through the trees.

Carol delved into her purse and came up with a small book clasped with a gold-plated band that ended in a lock. She also produced a key. "I brought you this," she said. "I had a feeling that it might be useful."

"What is it?" Ray asked, taking it from her hand.

"It's Dad's diary — his journal. They sent it to me with the rest of his things. I intended to burn it. But — what you said the other day at the house — about the killer and what he looked like —" She dropped off, then began all over. "I thought there might be some description in there. If he had the chance, Dad would have written it all down."

She gave over the key and Ray fit it into the tiny lock. It clicked and the clasp came open.

"Please, just the last entries," Carol asked. "The rest shouldn't be read."

Ray flipped the pages until he came to the last writing, then backtracked to the point where the professor had arrived at his vacation spot. The first entries were simple statements about the weather and his bad luck at fishing. They were short, only a paragraph each; but the next page Ray turned was full. His face lighted up as he scanned it and Will urged him to read it aloud. He began:

"'At last I have some company in the wilderness. A young man found his way here today and we have settled down together. He's good company, seeming quite intelligent and interested in everything I have to say. Though he isn't aware of it, I'm even more interested in him. There is something different about this man. I sense something in the way he looks at me, as though there is more to him than meets the eye, something which he has so far found no way to express. He tells me he comes from Arkansas and has worked his way north. It is odd, since there is no trace of an accent in his speech. We spent most of the day talking about telepathy. He devours it avidly. If only some of my students were like him.

"'Wednesday. Ezekiel is still with me and I think he intends to stay. Today we walked about the lake and talked more of telepathy, unfortunately for me, since exercise makes his bad limp even worse. I insisted on looking at his leg and was surprised to find such a bad job of medical tinkering in this day and age. He has a scar that runs down the entire calf of his left leg, made by what must have been a gash to the bone; and if my diagnosis is correct, muscles and all were severed. His arm fared better, leaving only a scar. It was a fearful accident, from what he says. I've watched him all day, still with the feeling that the watching is mutual. He's waiting for something. He has the blackest eyes imaginable — like pieces of jet. He cuts a fine figure — I might even take him home to Carol.

"'Thursday. Today I had the world's most unique experience in telepathy. I was right about Ezekiel. He *is* different. Our talk had grown more and more into the lines of ESP; and he was insisting that animals can be contacted as well as humans. I didn't swallow that to his liking, *so he showed me!* I want this down perfectly for my records. He stood in the middle of our campsite, gazed about him at the woods which crowd our place; and remained silent that way for approximately two minutes. I watched him with impatience; but each time I started to speak, he gestured me down, staring at me curiously with his black eyes, which seemed to have sparked up with an inner light. Then it happened. From all sides little animals crept out of the woods. They encircled us — squirrels, rabbits, chipmunks — I even spotted one snake. They appeared to be unwilling — frightened — but they came. They focused on Ezekiel and remained motionless there. He ignored them and came back to me, saying, "Now do you believe me?" I had to say, "Yes." When I admitted it, he sat down beside me and the animals scurried off. I've never seen anything like it! He claims he can "control" animals. He even claims responsibility for keeping our camp free of mosquitoes. He says that he can sense the presence of animals before they sense him; and could, if he chose, make a dog obey a command from a goodly distance. It's rather a handy thing and might be valuable to our poor mailman.

"'Friday. Today we talked about me, mostly. Ezekiel delved into my knowledge as though life, itself, depended on it. I have convinced him to let me work with him, to find the limit to his power. *Here is a telepath who cannot be denied no matter how hard-nosed his critic!* But he's a different breed. He cannot read my thoughts; yet he knows my intentions. He claims; but has not demonstrated, that he could send *me* in circles, just as he did the animals. I've asked him to try, but he refuses. There haven't been any animals about since yesterday's incident. Oh, yes, there was one — a cat who strayed over from the cottages across the lake. Anyway, the cat took one look at Ezekiel and arched up, running home. I personally think he frightened it away deliberately, so he wouldn't have to argue with me. He has the strangest conglomeration of knowledge. He says he's quite good at gardening and farming, mathematics and history. He also has an almost illogical ability to quote from the Bible. I'm going to cut this vacation short — I'm that anxious to get home and put my free year to some really good use.'"

Ray cleared his throat and looked up from the page. "That's the last entry. It must have happened the next day."

Carol was quiet in the back seat, tears dripping silently down her cheeks. "It makes him seem alive to hear what he wrote," she said. "I'm sorry."

"There's nothing to be sorry about," Ray said.

"No," she said, "there's only one thing now, isn't there?" She raised her eyes to meet theirs, her face panicked, her voice high. "He described Peter Kiel — didn't he? Peter murdered my father and all the others." She collapsed, cradling her head in her hands. "How can I ever go home to him?" she moaned. "How can I let him touch me?"

Ray started the car, decided to take Carol home long enough to pack some things and then get her out of Kiel's house.

The convertible was in the drive when they arrived. Chips darted out of the car at the sight of his own house and trotted sedately to the doorstep. Ray went up alone, leaving Carol with Will. Kiel answered his ring, saw Ray recoil the slightest bit; and stepped outside as Chips swished his tail out of the snow and into the house.

"What's wrong?" Kiel asked. "Where's Carol?"

"I've come for her things," Ray blurted. There was little he could say to explain. "She wants to come with us."

"Nonsense," Kiel scoffed. His gaze went to the car and Ray turned to see Carol climbing out. She came forward slowly, then faster; and walked into the waiting circle of her husband's arms.

"Wait a minute, Carol," Ray began.

"I'm sorry," she interrupted, "but Peter wants his dinner. Thanks for the ride." She disappeared into the house and Kiel put on one of the nastiest smiles Ray had ever seen.

Will was sheepish as Ray settled in the car. "I couldn't keep her here — she was determined to go to him."

"He's got her charmed," Ray said in disgust. "Let's get out of here."

Halfway home, Will said, "I think I've found the motive, Ray. No wonder it stumped us."

"Well?" Ray was still belligerent.

"Kiel gave us a hint the first time we met him. He told us to look for something the killer had taken from his victims. It's clear now. *He took their knowledge.* Grayson said Ezekiel was good at farming — that was the Mason woman. He was good at math and history — those were the Babcocks. The Bible — that came from the preacher and his wife. Come closer to the present and you'll find that he now knows everything that Carol's father knew, plus what the writer knew, the social behavior of the playboy; and the politics of the senator."

"And Jenny Peck?" Ray asked.

"Jenny was simply put out of the way. Her brain was normal. He didn't take anything from her."

CHAPTER FOURTEEN

"What can we do about it?" was the next question; and there was only one step to be taken. Ray and Will went to the police to identify Kiel as the killer. The police chief was a big man in girth and voice, with the square head and features of a one-time athlete. He looked at them out of the corner of his eye as they told their story; as he listened, his smile grew.

When Ray finished, intentionally omitting the weird facts and sticking to the physical description, the chief shook his head, grunting. "Amateur detectives! I've never heard a more fantastic story. If you had named anyone else, I might have listened to part of it; but to call Peter Kiel a killer —!"

*****

The phone was ringing when Ray and Will disconsolately returned home. It was Carol calling and she said, "Peter wants you and Will to come to dinner tonight. Can you make it?"

"No," Ray said hastily.

"But he wants to talk to you. He told me to be firm."

Ray covered the mouthpiece and relayed the invitation. Will shrugged. "Why not? It's crazy enough that he's walking the streets in broad daylight. We need proof — he's got it. Let's see what he wants."

*****

The winter sun had already disappeared when Ray and Will sent out at six-thirty for the Kiels'. Ray's stomach clenched tight, leaving no room for anything but fear. In his pocket rested the two small items of proof — the button and the sleeve patch.

Will sat humped beside him, his long legs pulled up close to the car seat. It was strange to Will that he suddenly found himself thinking of Kiel in adjectives normally reserved for animals. If Kiel weren't human — Earth human — then he wasn't a man; but something else, masquerading in borrowed clothes, with borrowed thoughts and borrowed knowledge.

Carol met them at the door, Chips in her arms, explaining that their maid had left without notice and the cook had followed.

"Then we're alone in the house," Ray remarked.

"Yes, but we'll be fine," Carol said. She looked exceptionally alert and bright; and Ray wondered how much of it was real. "Peter's in the living room," she told them. "You go on in and I'll see what's doing in the kitchen."

Kiel stood to meet them, extending his hand in welcome. The Christmas tree behind him seemed out of place. "Sit down. Or if you'd rather, Carol has your gifts under the tree. I don't think she'd mind if you opened them."

"After dinner, maybe," Will suggested. "Right now I'd like a drink."

When Kiel handed the glasses around, Ray took a sip, then straightened and took another, letting it linger on his tongue, tasting. It was a taste he hadn't known for months.

"Is there anything wrong with it?" Kiel asked.

"You're only the second man I've known who made this special drink," Ray answered. "The other was Professor Grayson. It was supposedly his invention."

"You're quite right," Kiel said. "I learned it from Carol."

Carol came through the side door then and went to the tree, returning with two gifts smothered in fancy bows, one for Ray and one for Will. "Here," she said, smiling. "Open them. I want to see you do it."

Ray glanced at her sourly, angry that she should appear so happy. He tore the bow from the package roughly, asking, "You're in good spirits. Something must have happened."

"It did." Carol went back to Kiel, catching his hand in hers. "I have an exciting future to plan on, now. Peter and I have decided to have a baby."

Ray ripped a sticker from the package. "Congratulations," he said, and added lowly, "*if* you can."

Kiel turned abruptly to business, all the friendliness gone. "I had a rather interesting phone call this afternoon. It was from a friend of mine — the chief of police."

"He told you why we went to see him?" Ray was angry with himself for not outguessing the chief's reaction.

"He did. You told him quite a story, didn't you? Just how far have you gone with this theory of yours?"

"Far enough," Ray countered, matching Kiel's pitch.

"I've been waiting," Kiel said flatly. "I knew you'd catch up sooner or later. God knows, you had enough clues — just not enough sense to put them together."

The sarcasm bit at Ray and something else grabbed at his mind, heightening his anger beyond reason until his hand twitched and shoved itself into his pocket, searching for the two small things that lay heavy there. He drew out the piece of cloth and the button.

"These clues we put together fast, Kiel. Here's your Christmas present." Kiel came the necessary distance and held out his hand. Ray dropped the two small articles and sat back, waiting for the explosion.

Kiel turned the things over on his palm, viewing them casually, making no attempt to pretend he didn't recognize them. Then he smiled, a condescending, pitying smile.

"So, the amateur detectives found themselves some tangible evidence," he said, laughing. "Artifacts looming from the past to tie the loose ends. Now isn't this something? And what conclusions have you drawn from two damning things like these?"

"Maybe more conclusions than you're ready to face." Ray didn't attempt to hold back any longer but gave way to the anger that pounded at his temples, seeing the same reaction in Will. Will's lanky body was a shaft of belligerence. "We know what you are, Kiel. *What* you are — not who."

Kiel's laughter died abruptly. "Maybe I should sit down and let you tell me the whole story. It should be amusing."

"Save us the trouble." Will didn't want to explain the weak theories word by word in front of the man. "There's an easier way for you to learn what we know."

"Oh? Are you considering suicide?"

"We know the story from the beginning — from the unfortunate man who saw the 'thing' pass by him in the air and was sick with the vileness of what he sensed inside, to the unfortunate girl who caught a glimpse of that same vileness but couldn't run far enough to escape. All we need now is help, and we can get that."

"Where?" Kiel's voice was mocking. "Two months ago I might have been worried, but not now. Little men can't frighten me any more — and you're a little man."

Carol had remained silent, a terrible blankness masking her face. Now she questioned: "Peter, what are you talking about?"

"Have you forgotten who this man is, Carol?" Ray snapped. "He murdered your father. And all the others."

"I wouldn't call it murder," Kiel said matter-of-factly. "I needed those people. They had a purpose and they served it."

"The children too?" Will demanded.

"The children especially." His tone held no emotion.

"McGregor was right. He said you could draw people to you but didn't have the decency to know what to do with them."

"I don't draw people," Kiel smiled. "They come to me. They're attracted. Do you know what your race is, Dr. Harper? It's a race of lemmings. They're attracted to me by the very things they fear —

strength, power, ruthlessness. They flock about me begging for destruction."

"What do you think you are?" Will snapped. "A god?"

Kiel sobered and his voice rose to dominate. "I *am* a god among your kind! Do you want me to prove it?"

Carol sensed the danger without understanding it and reached for him. "Peter! Don't hurt them!"

"I won't touch them," he sighed. "I'm through with that."

Ray pushed on with the point. "How can one man consider himself so powerful?"

"Simply because I am not *one* man," Kiel said. "I am many men — hundreds of men. And the longer I remain and the more people I meet, the more powerful I become. Alone I have certain force, but it's a circle. The more minds I control, the more minds I *can* control. I gain power from them — the power to control more and send myself farther. One day I can rule this planet and send myself far enough to contact my own race. There are millions of minds here — unlimited power."

"And that's what you're planning?" Ray got to his feet with an urge to put a stop to it right then. Will stood beside him and they faced Kiel together.

Kiel pushed Carol away and motioned toward Chips, his eyes never moving from the two men. "Take the cat upstairs," he said quickly. Carol hesitated, and he commanded: "Do as I say."

Carol gathered Chips in her arms and rushed away without question. As she disappeared, Kiel relaxed. "Let's not be violent, gentlemen," he said. "There's no use, I assure you. You've come this far; let's talk about it sensibly."

A quick coolness settled over Ray, relaxing tense muscles, pulsing with his blood and quieting his heart. He was too surprised to wonder at it and sat down.

"You've told us much," Will warned from his chair.

"I could tell you everything there is to know about myself and my plans and it would do you no good," Kiel said. "Please understand one thing. This town is mine! It does what I say, when I say. And I know your people. To control one of your towns is to control all of them. You see, I die hard; and if I die, I take hundreds with me."

"Do you mean you've taken control of everyone?" Will asked.

"The important ones are mine."

"Then they're nothing more than robots, waiting for you to give an order?" Ray winced at the thought.

"It isn't that way at all. They aren't even aware of the situation. You're really quite laughable, Dr. Harper." Kiel's attention darted to Will. "You must take care with that imagination. Look at your friend. Does he look like a robot to you?"

Ray turned, confused. "Of course not, but he isn't under —"

"But he is!" Kiel interrupted. "I can put him deeper if you don't believe me. I can make him into a robot."

"Don't you try it," Will threatened.

"You see?" Kiel smiled. "He doesn't even know what he is."

"And I don't believe it," Ray rose again.

Suddenly Will walked over and pushed Ray back. "Sit down, you're making a fool of yourself. You can't touch him."

"What's the matter with you?" Ray growled.

"I said sit down!" Will insisted. "Do I have to force you?"

Ray met Kiel's mocking eyes and conceded, "All right, Kiel. I see your point."

"But you're satisfied too soon." He looked at Will calmly. "Walk around the chair, Will."

Will stretched his long legs and proceeded to walk stiffly around the chair, his face a blank mask of itself.

He circled round and round and Kiel began to laugh. "Look at him. I've never seen anything like it. Doesn't he look like a perfect idiot? I could have an army of them."

"That's enough!" Ray shuddered. "I believe you."

Immediately, Will halted. He was himself again, only more subdued.

"Let him go, Kiel," Ray pleaded.

"Why?" Kiel asked softly. "Now that I have him, why should I let him go?" His eyes were bland on Ray. "I can't have a threat hanging over me all the time; now can I?" As Ray's hands clenched into fists, he added, "You're given to more action than your friend. Maybe I chose the wrong one."

Ray started to protest; but a coldness crept over him, numbing him. He fought to resist and failed. He could feel his bones stretched inside his body and his muscles ached with unordered strain. His mind was a cloud of black that refused to translate the world for him. Underneath the cold there was a constant trembling, a struggling to escape a bond that was unseen but felt. The "I" of him was prisoner while someone else ordered his body. Then it muted into coolness, soft and pliant; and he found himself sitting in his original place. Will was staring at him, his mouth wide open.

"You put up quite a fight," Kiel congratulated. "You don't like being a pawn, do you?" They faced him with doubt and he added, "Relax. You're free of me, now."

"You haven't any soul," Ray stated bluntly. "Is that how you committed those murders? Just with your mind?"

"You don't want a demonstration of that too?"

Ray and Will remained silent. Carol returned then, glanced at the three men quizzically, then sat down near Kiel without saying a word.

"I didn't touch one of those people with my hands," Kiel said, addressing his wife as well as the two men. "I didn't need to touch them. Your people do not suspect, so they have no defense. The weak I don't waste time with. I know they are mine whenever I want them. The strong I have to fight. So far I have won."

Ray jumped in on the end of his words: "Why have you left us alone until tonight? Even when we are so dangerous to you? Where do we fit into your classifications of weak and strong?"

"Obviously weak." Will admitted it. "He took us without any trouble."

"I did," Kiel stated. "But that was the first challenge. You might have fought back after the reaction wore off. I've waited for you because I suspected you were two of the strong ones and I had enough on my hands. Now it suits me to let you go your own way and see how far that is. I have plans for you."

"Why can't I move?" Will pounded his fists on the chair. "Why can't I *do* something?"

"Kiel has a hand in that," Ray muttered.

"What good would violence accomplish?" Kiel asked. "You've come so far I don't want to stop you short of understanding. I've forced you into the open so that we can drop all pretense. I'm free to operate on my own terms with you and Carol. And I have the chance to test my groundwork and discover any flaws. I'm sure you'll point them out to me."

"In other words, we're still just tools as far as you're concerned," Ray spat.

"How could you be anything else?"

"But you said you would leave us alone." Will's fear of returning to the robot state clouded his voice.

"I meant that," Kiel assured him. "I want you to keep your initiative, to do your best against me, whether you can understand it or not."

"Do we have to listen to any more of this?" Ray demanded. "Are you going to force us to sit here and let you make fools of us, or can we leave?"

"Leave, of course, if you wish. I wouldn't think of forcing you."

Ray tried his legs and found them steady, willing to answer his commands and hold him. He went to the hall without another word, Will close behind.

"I suppose I can expect some retribution," Kiel said, opening the door. "Try; I'll be waiting." And as they started down the walk, he called: "Merry Christmas. And don't lose touch."

The door slammed, cutting his laughter in two; and Ray and Will stepped into the fresh, reviving air of the snowy outdoors.

Kiel was awesome; Kiel was alien. It was hard to realize it looking at him, but he had come from the stars — a man who had traveled space and walked on strange worlds.

For centuries the Earth had waited for such a man — a man from another planet, another universe — a man intelligent, advanced. But in one important, dreadful way Kiel was not a man. For the Earth had awaited a civilized man, and Kiel was not civilized. Kiel was a brutal killer.

Ray forced his mind to hover on that blunt fact and forget the awe.

*****

"All right — this is what you were talking about before, isn't it?" Carol asked Kiel quietly after he had closed the door on the retreating figures of her two friends. "Control, challenge, middlemen. No wonder I couldn't understand."

Kiel's black eyes swung to her and rested there a moment. Her mask and tension had partially disappeared; her shell was full. She realized it; and contentment crept through her body, making her stretch.

"You feel more yourself now," he said.

"Much more. It's the difference in you, isn't it?"

He nodded. "It's all in the open, where I want it."

"Not really," she insisted. "I don't really know you at all, Peter. You're more a stranger than ever. You'll never know how odd it is to realize you're married to someone who isn't even a — a man — as you know men. I don't know what to think."

"I can fix that — if you want to hear. It has been lonely, keeping it to myself. Come here, beside me."

She moved into place for want of any excuse but didn't close the distance between them, holding a little away. He began talking, describing the planet he knew as home, painting word pictures for her.

He told of a planet much like Earth, but where the men were different. Each of them was invested with a power of mind, and each used that power to his own advantage or fell to others. From birth, mothers hid their children away until their faculties had begun to develop, praying that their child would be a strong one. If the child was strong, he survived the inroads made upon him by other children and adults as he was tested and sought by each person he met. He learned the tricks and the codes, preparing himself. If the child was weak, he was soon in the control of another, serving his wishes, living the life of a slave. Nothing and no one mattered. Only the preservation of the personal ego and the domination of others to maintain that ego. There was only Self. There was no room for compassion, only appraisal; no room for sensitivity, only alertness; no room for ease, only cunning.

Kiel's own dominance over forty men put him in a high bracket, subject only to demands and attacks from those above him. It also allowed him the temporary freedom of traveling alone into space as a scout, the chance to rest, away from the constant parry and thrust of mental power.

"The crash seemed the end of the world," he said, "until I realized that this planet was rich in minds and that the minds were so easy to come by. I can be anything I want to be. I can rule this world."

"And you intend to," she added for him.

"I do," he admitted simply. "And I want you with me. Now that you know the truth, how do you feel? Am I repulsive?"

She stared hard at him, into the black eyes that were strangely softened, and said, "I don't yet know how I feel. I should hate you, shouldn't I?"

"Do you?"

She didn't answer, testing her emotions. "Why can't I think clearly?" she cried at last. "Are you still guiding my mind?"

"Not enough to interfere. Perhaps you're not completely reoriented. This has been an ordeal for you and it will take time to recover."

"So?" she watched him.

"So — I'll wait. When you know, I'll know. All I ask is that you act the part of my wife when other people are about until you decide. Otherwise, I'll have to 'help' you. It's important, Carol — to me and to you. I can wait."

CHAPTER FIFTEEN

Kiel, as an individual threat, didn't worry Ray too much. But the prospects he had outlined of contacting others of his race was frightening.

Kiel was a cancer, spreading out one cell at a time, until he wove a strangle hold on the body, until his position was so great that the body could no longer fight but only tolerate him and finally die. And by attacking the heart of the body, the men who gave orders to other men, he had entrenched himself.

Ray went along with Will, who insisted on doing the obvious first. They gathered the bits of evidence and returned to police headquarters. But again they got nowhere. The chief wouldn't even consider the possibility that their story was true.

Ray stamped through the door in a maddened fury, but he finally admitted, "I don't suppose the chief can help it — not when he doesn't even know he's a robot."

Then they went to the FBI office. The girl behind the desk was polite and smiling.

"Sorry," Ray said. "We'd like to see your boss."

"He's not in right now."

"One question, Miss," Will asked. "Do you know a man named Peter Kiel? Has he ever been up here?"

"Peter Kiel?" she brightened. "Of course. He drops in every now and then. He's a fine man."

"Thanks," Will sighed. "We won't bother to wait. Your boss wouldn't be interested in our business."

*****

At home at dinner Will shrugged. "There aren't any holes. He's covered the law agencies, the newspapers, the television and radio stations. No one will move. What's next?"

"We'll have to make some holes, that's all. And it has to be *now* — or we'll be too late."

"What do we do with him, Ray? Suppose we get help? What will happen? No jail could hold him because there's always a man with a key. He couldn't be tried or executed. What are we trying to do? Get our hands physically on him?"

"Of course," Ray said flatly.

"Then do you know what you're saying?"

Ray stared at his plate, his angular face squaring itself in determined lines. "There's only one way to stop Peter Kiel, Will, whether we like the idea or not. We have to kill him."

"No!" Will pushed away from the table.

"What do you mean, no?" Ray shouted. "Surely, you've known that all along. Kiel knows it."

"Until now I've pictured exposing him for what he is and letting the law take its course. I just didn't consider the idea that stopping him would mean murder!"

"Don't call it murder. Call it extermination. He doesn't go by any rules. You and I — we've never thought in those terms, but now we have no choice. And no help. This has to be done."

Will came back to the table, his body stiff and slow-footed. "Then we just take a gun and go out there. We shoot him and get it over with and go to jail for his murder."

"We wouldn't through the front door. But if we can find enough men who are not under Kiel's thumb — men like McGregor, for instance — then we can go together. Maybe Kiel can't handle many at once. When he's gone, the men in control will return to their senses and believe our evidence."

"You intend to attack his house," Will stated. "I can't help it, Ray, I feel detached — as if this were something in a movie and I'm not actually in it. If *I* feel that way, how are you going to convince men like McGregor?"

"Mac won't need much convincing; and if we can dig up only four or five more, it will be enough."

*****

The day after Christmas was usually a let-down day. But this time, it was heightened for Ray. It was a day of intense explaining and persuading. He faced Will's reaction all over again in McGregor.

"There's no help, Mac," Ray persuaded. "We've reached the end. There are only the two of us. Will and I could wash our hands of it easily enough, but then there would be no one."

Mac clutched his pipe. "I'm not a young man, Ray. Even if I wanted to do this thing, I'm not sure I'm physically able."

"I'm not asking you to fight," Ray explained. "Just to add to our number."

"The whole thing is incongruous. I can't quite stomach it." He tapped his pipe, emptying good, unlit tobacco. Ray let him think it out. "Since I believe you," Mac said after five minutes of silence, "and since Kiel is such a menace, I'll have to say yes. It's not what I want to do, you understand."

"I know. It's what you have to do. Thanks, Mac."

McGregor scribbled some lines on a scrap of paper. "I've got two men in mind to bring in with us. Jerry Bacon — he won several decorations in the war and he's a science-fiction writer, so he's prepared. I think I can convince him. Then there's Carl Empers. He's the type of man you need — anything for excitement." Mack lifted himself disgustedly out of his chair and sighed. "Here I am enlisting the aid of a man I've always abhorred and for the very reason I've abhorred him."

"Can you handle them yourself?"

"I can." Mack was resigned.

"Then bring them to my place tomorrow night at seven, and we'll plan our moves."

Ray went from Mac's to one of the dormitories, devoid of students for the holiday, except for the few who had no place to go. Jean Dereau was one of those. Since he had such strong feelings stemming from the time he claimed Kiel had stolen something from him, he was easy to convince.

*****

The living room filled at the scheduled hour, and Ray had his first glimpse into the sensations Will and McGregor had tried to explain. Now that the time had come, it did seem unreal, as though he were standing outside in a dream.

Jerry Bacon was a wiry young man with horn-rimmed glasses and a look of grave concentration. Carl Empers, on the other hand, was elated, his pale face split by an excited smile. He didn't believe the facts about Kiel, but had convinced himself that he did to give him an excuse to attack.

They drew circles on the map to indicate where each man would place himself. One side of the house had the natural barrier of water. Of the other three, the front was too close to the street, so it was eliminated. The sides of the house were flanked by garden and wall. They could approach without notice by neighbors and without an alarm.

There were only two guns. Ray kept one for himself; Will insisted on taking the other.

They decided to take two cars. They would park one well away from Kiel's house and bring the other nearby, ready in case they needed it. The men were to come up separately, walk along the sidewalk, and climb the wall into the grounds. Mac volunteered to be the bait. He would leave the car at nine o'clock, cross the street, and knock on Kiel's garden door in the guise of a delivery man. He would ask for Kiel and refuse to go inside. When Kiel came to the door, that would be the moment for attack, while he was framed in the light.

*****

Ray followed Will from the sidewalk, over the wall, and into the deep snow of the grounds, his stomach gnawing with anxiety threatening to eat away his backbone.

They stepped from shadow to shadow where moonlight patched the snow with deep greys against white. It was quiet. Snow muffled every sound and the river was frozen, its running stilled. They crept on without sight of their fellows, gaining cover from barren bushes and clumps of fir trees.

The house loomed up, lighted only in the downstairs windows. The light of the Christmas tree gleamed onto the snow in splotches of red and green. When they had reached the cover of the garden wall, Ray's watch said five minutes to nine. He caught Will's sleeve and pulled down.

"We'll wait here till Mac makes his move," Ray whispered. He drew out the gun, looking toward the door where Kiel would appear. "Where's your gun?" he asked Will.

"I gave it to someone else," Will answered. "There was no sense in having them both on the same side of the house."

The slam of the car door brought them up stiffly. Mac was starting his walk to the house. He was a black shadow in the moonlight, rather bedraggled in smudged work clothes, his gait nervous. Ray crouched, readying his muscles for the moment.

Mac strode up the driveway. Three steps later, a wild bark and growl split the silence and a great shape streaked around the house straight for Mac. Another dog joined in the cry at the far side, and shouts came from the men as they tried to protect themselves from the hairy shapes. Mac toppled under the leap of the dog, arms flailing. At the same moment the lights went on in the house.

Ray darted for Mac, reached his side, and grabbed the dog by its chain collar. He yanked back and the dog lifted on its hind legs. Mac jumped up, clutching the heavy wool scarf that had saved his throat, grabbed the chain, and forced the animal to crouch. Held from the back, the dog was helpless; and Mac was in control. Growls still echoed from the other side as Ray stumbled through the snow to Will.

"What now?" Will shouted. "Do we go in?"

Ray hesitated only a moment. "We have to!"

They dashed for the house, stumbling in the drifts piled against bushes and rocks. The last open space loomed before them when the screech of tires broke the air, drowning the barking and the shouts. Flashing red lights shot up in the street and yelling men jumped from cars, spreading out as they ran. Ray pulled Will back and they sprinted for cover behind the wall.

"Don't shoot!" Ray yelled, hoping the man with Will's gun would hear.

The police rushed to surround the house, then turned in unison to face outward, and began a strange, slow march forward, as though flushing an animal. They all had guns in hand; and suddenly they opened fire, pouring out rays of bullets in a wide circle.

"What are they doing?" Will screamed.

"Get out of here!" Ray shouted, leaping backward, searching for cover. The policemen came on in their fantastic slow-gaited circle, guns spiting, flashing orange.

"They don't know what they're doing," Ray yelled. "Jerry! Mac! Carl!" he called at the top of his voice. "Get out! The car! The car!"

They scrambled back the way they had come, taking three steps at a dead run, then crouching behind a tree. A fan of bullets rained behind them. The police weren't aiming, just shooting.

They ran in plain sight of the lights and the men but weren't chased. The police plodded on, faces blank, legs stiff, loading and firing. Ray reached the street and made a dash for the car. Mac was inside with the motor going.

"Ready?" Mac called.

"No!" Ray pushed him away from the wheel, taking over himself. "We've got to wait for the others."

"But the cops will be in the street any minute," Mac shouted. The edge of the circle of policemen was approaching the sidewalk. Some of their bullets ploughed into their own cars at the curb.

Ray shoved the gear into reverse. "Duck!" he yelled. "I'm going for the others."

He stamped his foot on the gas and the car leaped backward, speeding the distance to the house and through the line of fire. He braked and slid ten feet on ice, fighting to end up facing the other direction.

He blew the horn frantically to signal the other men. One figure leaped the garden wall, then another. They crouched over, zigzagging for the safety of the car. It was Jerry Bacon and Carl Empers.

They jammed into the back with Will. "Where's Jean?" Ray demanded.

"He's dead." Jerry's voice was hollow. "He ran into one of the cops and got it full face. He turned the cop around when he fell and the damned fool walked back into the line of fire, himself, blasting all the way. Two cops are dead."

Ray stamped the accelerator. The car raced forward, down the twisting street, away from the noise. No one gave chase, but Ray sped on until he had put two miles between them and the police. Then he slowed to the speed limit.

"We gave Kiel too much time," he cursed. "He must have sensed us right away and called for the police."

"Since when do cops open fire without warning?" Empers growled from the back. "If I'd had a gun —"

"That would have been plain murder," Will protested. "They didn't know what they were doing."

"Who had the gun?" Ray asked.

"I did," Jerry said. "I didn't use one bullet. But I came close when I saw that kid die."

"You can't fight robots," Ray said through clenched teeth. "We could have stood there and picked them off one at a time if we'd wanted slaughter. We're responsible for three deaths anyway. They'll be looking for us now. I'm sorry."

"We all knew what we were doing," Mac said. "They might not know who it was, except that I've got a get a shot for a dog bite."

CHAPTER SIXTEEN

The papers carried the story. The article told of a young exchange student who had gone berserk and shot two policemen before he was killed himself. The policemen were described in terms of heroism: Jean Dereau was covered with black.

Kiel had chosen to release his own story, through the medium of *his* newspaper and *his* police department (the neighbors who had heard the commotion were probably under the same influence) and Ray and Will awoke as free men. But the frustration of knowing that Kiel was laughing at them was worse than being hunted.

McGregor put in an appearance. Puffing on his pipe, he ringed himself with a smoke screen, invited himself for coffee and opened a subject Ray hadn't considered. "Just how intelligent do you think Kiel is?"

"That's a hard thing to say," Ray said, frowning.

"And maybe not too important?" Mac smiled shyly. "I mean, since he has this power, he doesn't need brains? That's only one way of looking at it. There has to be a measure of the man, power or no power. Put his ability in the hands of a moron and we could get to him. But if he has us coming both ways — then we're in trouble."

"Why any more than we already are?" Will asked.

"Because he's probably out guessed us all the way. You say he's leaving you alone. That suggests that he has no fear of you because he knows your capabilities. It's a simple test of his defenses for him. And as he said, amusement.

"The way I see it," Mac continued, "Kiel is probably far beyond us in intelligence. He has the ability to do more than one thing at a time. He can co-ordinate his robots in one corner of his mind while he plans ahead and lives in his own present. He can watch you as a man watches a child's efforts to murder him with a rubber sword. He simply isn't afraid of you."

"What are you getting at?" Ray demanded.

"I'm saying that you'll have to accept your role as harmless puppets, act it out, and go on from there. It's an ironic fact that men with their minds on complex things tend to overlook little things. All of the absent-minded professor tales are based on this. So if you behave as he expects, let him relax in his own preplanned way, then you may be able to catch him off guard. Even the beekeeper sometimes gets stung — by a bee he sits upon."

The phone's jangle interrupted; and when Ray answered, he heard Carol's voice in that familiar request: Would he and

Will come out that evening for dinner?

Mac urged him to accept. "You can't overlook any opportunity to meet with him. It's your chance to put his mind at rest and make him think you're falling into his expected pattern. Take it."

Ray yielded to the only one with a plan and told Carol they would come.

"It's probably revenge," Will offered. "Maybe we should take a gun and finish it now."

"No!" Mac exploded. "This man is not going to be trapped by overt action. He has to be tricked, not attacked. If only I could go along — You say he's more than willing to talk about himself and answer questions. I've got questions to be asked."

"Come, then," Ray said. "There won't be any objection. But you'll be taking the chance of becoming a robot."

"I'm not afraid of him," Mac stated steadfastly. "You've got yourself a date."

*****

As they waited on the steps of Kiel's house, Mac whispered: "Now remember, no antagonizing, no insinuating. You said he thinks he's a god; well, push his pedestal up a little higher until the view down gets hazy."

The addition of an extra guest caused no disturbance except to make Carol nervous. She looked rather harassed from the wild night before. Kiel shook hands cordially, not even attempting to hide his amusement.

Ray sat down with Chips and stroked the striped head. The cat was getting thin from his constant watching and Ray wished he could take him out of the house.

The three men waited, wondering how long Kiel would keep up the polite chatter before he swung to a mention of their attempt against him. But he was enjoying his position and basking in Carol's attention. If Ray had harbored any doubts about Carol's emotions, they were gone now; she hovered about her husband, making a fool of herself, Ray thought.

Ray understood the excitement Mac was feeling. Mac was seeing Kiel first for the thing he was — a man from the stars — and wondering what strange things he could relate if only he would.

If was when they were sipping their second cocktail that Kiel opened up. "That was quite a show you put on last night, Ray. 'Storming the fort,' I believe is the correct title for it."

"We all know it was a stupid move, so don't point it up," Ray muttered.

"It was the natural thing," Kiel admitted. "But who were your confederates?"

"Don't try to tell me you don't know," Ray scoffed.

"I was one," Mac spoke up, meeting Kiel's sizing eyes with the measure of his own. "I met one of the dogs, unfortunately."

"They made a successful delaying action. But you surprise me, Dr. McGregor. I wouldn't have expected a man of your age and intelligence to engage in commando tactics."

"That's what I told them," Mac laughed. "What surprised me, if I'm allowed a surprise, is how you knew we were there at all. Do you read minds?"

Kiel looked at him sideways. "No, I don't read minds. I read intentions, if anything."

"Intentions?"

"Pretences, emotions, motives. I can sense the changes in your brain pattern, the heightening or tightening when you are excited — the changes which occur with your emotions. You might say I'm a walking electroencephalograph."

"Then you can't tell what I'm thinking right now?" Mac let amazement flow into his tone.

"I'm not a telepath," Kiel admitted. "But from this moment on, I will be able to identify you out of a hundred people. You have a distinct pattern which separates you from the rest. You might say you have just now met me."

Mac's eyes glinted with interest. "And when you take control of a man, what happens then? Do you project yourself into him?"

"In a way. I capture his brain pattern and turn it back, altering it where I choose. I take out and put in. I force my pattern into his mold and run his body for him. I can take into myself whatever a man possesses in his mind and then it becomes mine. Unfortunately, this can't be done without violence. I could reach out and take one small particle of information from you and all you would feel would be a headache. But if I wanted something bigger, something deeper, you would be destroyed. Don't ask me why skulls split open — that I don't know, myself, except that the brain swells to a tremendous size and pressure before it shrinks and that probably cracks the shell."

"It's amazing," Mac sighed. "When put in unemotional terms, it's not quite so horrible, is it?"

The maid announced dinner. Kiel went ahead with Carol and Ray fell back a moment to demand an explanation of Mac's actions. Mac waved him aside impatiently, "Don't spoil it now. Just listen and remember what you hear. The man's an egotist — he'll deliver himself into our hands because of it."

Mac continued at the table. "What about animals then? Do they actually have enough brain power to be controlled?"

"Of course. I tried to explain this to Ray, but he wouldn't listen. I can control any animal."

"Except cats," Ray interjected.

"Yes, except cats."

"Why is that?" Mac acted the role of a curious codger.

"Cats have a one-track mind, to put it simply. They decide something and they're too stubborn to change. Chips, in there, has lived with me all this time and still refuses to submit. He's proud and vain — if you'll excuse the human adjectives — and he won't give in to me. He quite simply hates me."

"Are cats abler than people then?"

"I didn't say that," Kiel hurried to explain. "It's just that people, with their complexities, can be lured, cajoled, and tricked. I can be upon them before they're aware of danger. Chips was on the alert the moment I came within his range, and he doesn't relax as long as I stay in range. He transmits a constant stream of one strong emotion, and I can't get through to him. It's like jamming on radio waves. He disrupts my pattern."

"So that's the reason," Carol gasped. Kiel shot her a fast warning glance and she looked down at her plate.

"Chips and I wage a battle every now and then," he continued. "Mostly, I leave him alone. But I'm afraid Carol's going to have to give him up. You noticed how thin he's getting. I don't like to see that. I admire his courage."

Mac said meekly, "You know, Mr. Kiel, it's a strange sensation sitting here beside you and knowing that I am completely helpless — that at any moment I might not be myself any more. It must give you a feeling of great power."

"I have great power," Kiel answered simply. "I don't think about it one way or another."

"In a way, it might be a pleasant thing," Mac mused, "just to live and enjoy living and let someone else do the deciding. It might not be so bad for humanity, after all."

"Mac!" Ray exploded. "That's —"

"No, no," Mac said, cutting him off. "After all, if it's going to come, we may as well think of the good side of it."

Kiel's eyes were suddenly wary, fastened on him like suction cups. "You don't mean a word of that, McGregor. What are you trying to do?"

"Frankly, I'm trying to protect myself, to cross myself off your list as an adversary. You can't blame me for that."

"But I haven't threatened you." Kiel appeared perplexed. "In fact, I rather admire you. You remind me a good deal of Carol's father; and since you were such friends, I have a good estimation of you already, through his eyes."

"It's eerie," Mac said and shivered. "If you remove your own personality and the others which succeeded Grayson, would you then *be* Grayson? And I could talk to you as Grayson?"

"Yes."

"It's like resurrecting the dead."

"I owe much to him," Kiel said. "He opened the world for me. Up until then, I was stifled by superstitions and feeble minds. I was shut inside. But his mind was closer to my own; and with it, I burst out." He cast his attention down the table to Ray and Will. "As much as I enjoy talking to you, it's stirring up too much emotion in your friends. You think I've planned some sort of revenge, don't you, Ray?"

Ray didn't answer but violently sawed off a piece of meat with his knife.

"Don't bait him, Peter," Carol asked. "You invited them here, don't start something. Please."

Kiel raised his wine glass in a mock toast to her and said nothing more.

The talk dragged on until they put a voluntary end to it. Kiel showed them out; and as they started away, called: "Don't be discouraged. The battle isn't too uneven, actually. I've given myself a handicap. You should be grateful." The door closed on the beginning of his low laugh.

Ray didn't know if he was angry with Mac or no, and Will echoed his thoughts. "You've just about taken this over, haven't you?" he asked Mac.

Mac shrugged his tweed-covered shoulders. "I suppose I have. But that's because I have a plan. The man with a plan always leads, right?" Will didn't respond. "You don't care, do you?"

"No, I don't care. If you actually have a plan, I'm with you."

"Then I'll tell you what I think," Mac said, refilling his pipe. "Kiel has this town sewed up — maybe even this state — but he hasn't gotten to Washington. Our help has to come directly from there. Well, I have a connection big enough to get some help. He's an old friend — Henry Neilson. He's sharp, shrewd, not afraid of the Devil, and in an executive position with the FBI. He'll come out if I saw him."

"Can you make him believe the story?" Will questioned.

"I can try. I'll call him tonight if we're agreed."

"Agreed," Ray said, bobbing his head.

"Agreed," Will submitted.

Mac's face was ruddy with the thought of action. "You watch. We'll put an end to this yet." He went out the door, a belated Christmas carol whistling from his mouth: "God rest ye, merry gentlemen, let nothing you dismay."

CHAPTER SEVENTEEN

Henry Neilson was unconvinced by the story that Ray, Will and Dr. McGregor told him. And the three men with him were the same. So Mac made a hurried call to be sure Kiel was where he was reported to be — at a reception in the capital building — took Neilson in tow, and set out to crash the party.

When they returned two hours later, Neilson wasn't incredulous any more. He faced Ray and demanded: "One question. Is there absolutely no hope of getting the man on our side?"

"None," Ray replied surely.

"Then he has to be eliminated," Neilson said, bobbing his head as though it were the rap of a sentencing gavel. "He's infuriating. I don't like anyone who can make me look so insignificant."

"Kiel laughed when I introduced Hank with all his titles," Mac explained. "He said, 'Welcome into the fold,' and laughed."

"Maybe I'm foolish," Neilson growled, "but I'm not used to being considered so unimportant that the man I'm after openly challenges me."

"That's what we've been up against. You're supposed to have some ideas," Will snapped.

Neilson rubbed his chin. "It's obvious that violence isn't the answer. We could blow him out of existence if he was the only one involved. But we can't endanger the men he controls, that would be mass slaughter. And we can't do it by force of numbers, because we can't let this news out to the public."

"Why not?" Ray asked.

"Panic, young man, panic."

"You government men are always afraid of panic," Ray countered. "You just say the word and close the door."

"All right." Neilson grew stubborn. "People stay off the streets and report banging shutters when they only suspect a *murderer* is about. What will they do if you tell them that this man, with his power, is among them? Panic!"

With Ray's surrendering shrug, Neilson left the room to phone Washington. A half-hour later, he returned, took a stance, and said, "This is official government business now. My orders are to get the job done but to protect all innocent people."

"So?" Mac asked.

"So, since I can't use force of numbers, I'm enlisting the three of you. An army of four isn't much; but if we use our brains, it may serve. We need some organization. First, I want my men to meet

Kiel so that they know whom they're after. Then, I want a systematic grilling, secretly, of any and all officials we might use — including the men on campus. We need a battery of brains. We can all work on that. Simple conversation should do the trick. If a man professes too much admiration for Kiel, cross him off."

*****

A meeting was arranged for the three agents. They met Kiel under the guise of boat enthusiasts trying to get neighborhood permission to use the river as a place for races. They came away sure that they hadn't fooled him.

Ray had eight physical examinations in order to question doctors, ten dental checkups, and violated traffic laws to get to police officers and judges. He checked off names one after another. When his list was completed, it was one big pencil scratch all the way down the page.

Will's list matched his. So did all the others. Kiel had the town wrapped up tight, and the state was going the same way.

Then a chance meeting with Kiel at a coffee shop sent Ray home fast. He burst into the living room, shouting at Neilson: "Where are your men? We haven't asked *them* the questions, have we?"

Neilson stamped to the stairway and called his men down.

"Don't prepare them," Ray commanded. "Ask them what they think of Peter Kiel, just as we've asked everybody else."

The three agents came in casually, staying in a group. Neilson sent two of them out and faced the one remaining. "This is out of my hands, Brown, so forgive me," he apologized. "I have to ask you a question. You've met Peter Kiel. What's your opinion of him? Actually?"

"I think this whole thing is a bunch of trash. He's a pretty fine man."

Neilson's fists clenched into hard balls and he had trouble controlling his voice as he sent Brown out. The other two men were called one at a time and they gave the same reply. They liked Kiel; he was a great man. Neilson immediately ordered them to pack.

"I'm ashamed!" Neilson's voice was vehement. "My own men."

"There's no reason to be ashamed," Ray muttered. "We've just made another mistake."

"What did he say to you?" Mac asked.

"He said thanks for bringing in government men. He said it saves him a trip. Now he has an 'in.' You're probably next, Neilson. Those men — and you — will go back to Washington and be there to help him when he comes, to introduce him into high places. It saves him some groundwork."

"The nerve of that man," Neilson growled. "I'll settle this by sending my men West. They won't return to Washington and neither will I, until this is over." His head jerked in apprehension. "Do you suppose I'm being controlled, too? Do you suppose he's got to me and I don't even know it?"

"My guess is," Mac put in, "that he's keeping you for last."

"And what do we do in the meantime?" Will asked. "Where does your plan go from here, Neilson?"

The doorbell chimed and Ray sputtered, "Sorry. This place is getting to be like Grand Central Station."

Carol stepping into the hall, her face anxious. "Well," Ray said, "this is a surprise. You haven't got Kiel with you, I hope."

"No," she murmured under her breath. "I'm leaving him, Ray. I can't stand it any more."

Ray had been waiting for those words, but now they seemed too secret to be spoken aloud.

"Why don't you say something?" she asked.

"Come into the living room," Ray said. "There's a man I want you to meet."

She stood straight in the archway, waiting to be introduced to Neilson, knowing who he was already. He pounced on her name, pricking up his ears to catch every word she uttered.

There was no way to be sure whether Carol had come for the reasons she stated or had been sent to them by Kiel. But trust had to begin somewhere. Ray filled her in on the details of Neilson's position.

"My position is so different from yours," she tried to explain. "Living with him — seeing him every day and sharing his life — it's hard to think of him in such drastic terms. My mind knows what he is and what he has done, but it won't quite accept it when I look at him. But that's over now. I'm leaving him."

"*Can* you leave him?" Will asked pointedly. "Will he let you?"

"He won't be able to stop me. I'll be gone when he gets home tonight." Her hazel eyes were sure and resolved.

"I'm glad you're getting out of there," Mac nodded. "This thing is bound to become violent and we'll have fewer compunctions with you out of the way."

"I don't know." Neilson sounded undecided. "A bird in the hand — You do know, Mrs. Kiel, that we're playing this game for keeps, don't you? That the ultimate end can only be the complete disability or destruction of your husband?"

"I know." Carol betrayed neither purpose nor horror.

"She's our answer." Neilson sucked in his lips, swinging to Ray. "You tried attacking from the outside. How about from the inside? Does your husband trust you, my dear?"

"He didn't at first; but since I know about him, he does."

"And you're a sensible girl," Neilson flattered.

"Of course, she is." Mac took over. "Your father was always proud of that, Carol — that, and your courage. Do you accept thoroughly the fact that Kiel has to be killed?"

Carol nodded, the beginning of anxiety on her face.

"Then," Mac stated firmly, "you're the one to do it."

Carol leaped to her feet, her body still in protest. "No! How can you even suggest it?"

"Call it a sacrifice, if you must, but you are the only one," Neilson parried. "You have his trust; you have access to him — what's keeping you back? Does he still have a hold on you?"

"No, he doesn't," Carol's hands partly covered her face. "But, don't you see, I've lived with him! I can't kill him!"

"Are you still in love with him?" Ray demanded.

"No!" she cried. "How could I be in love with him? I just don't know how I feel. I wish you'd leave me alone."

Ray didn't give her time to gather strength to refuse. He softened his tone and asked: "Carol, stop and think what your father would say if he were here. What would he do?"

"He'd tell me to do it. But, I tell you, I can't!"

"Because he's still got you under his thumb!" Ray shouted. "You can't do anything on your own. He'll let you run around, but there's always an end to your rope and he can jerk up on it anytime he chooses. You're living with a monster who cares nothing for you except as a means to an end — a convenience to satisfy his needs. You're letting yourself be used as a female animal and as a necessary chattel."

"Stop it!" she screamed, whirling on him, then wilted.

"And what about children?" Ray let the momentum of anger he had held back for months carry him. "Do you want his children? Little monsters who will take you over as soon as their brains coordinate enough to reach out for you?"

Carol stood in the one place, a waxy statue, tears streaming down her cheeks, her chest heaving. She reached out her arms to Mac and he gathered her in, stroking her head like a child's. "That's enough, Ray," he said.

"But he's right," Carol sobbed. "I know he's right. That's the trouble: I know it's all true; but I can't move."

"Are you willing to help us then?" Neilson asked.

"That's why I came," she cried, clutching Mac's shoulders.

"I can help you," Mac said and led her to the sofa. "I can rid you of whatever is holding you back. Will you let me?"

Carol nodded, but Ray asked for an explanation. Mac left the room with the three men. In the hall, he said, "I'm going to try hypnosis. She's willing to kill, so I only have to free her from the fear of it, and if I can, from any hold he has. She knows it's the right thing and I think she'll be able to do it."

*****

Night settled over the house. Carol turned on the Christmas tree lights, hearing the click of falling needles as she touched the drying branches. The house was quiet. The servants were out and she was alone with Kiel.

Carefully she mixed two drinks, her stomach in a tight knot. She walked about in a fog, realizing that Mac had helped her to that state.

A sense of danger pervaded the room; and beyond the hall door where there was no light, the shadows were menacing. She lifted Chips into her arms. He didn't want to remain, sensing the tension in her. She let him have his way and he curled up in his favorite chair, eyes unblinkingly on the dining room door.

Kiel came in and sat across from Carol, sipping his drink, his body relaxed and his eyes friendly. "You're upset about something, Carol. I can sense it."

"It's just the effect of this constant war," she covered. "I keep expecting to hear shots."

"No one will harm you. I promise you that."

She could think of nothing to say; the idea of what was ahead made words impossible. As he picked up the paper, she excused herself to clear the table.

In the dining room she leaned against the wall, breathing deeply to restore her calm. Her hands trembled and she was frightened. She consciously stiffened her back and went to the chest where she had hidden the gun. It was set and loaded. She raised it up and her lips moved silently as she said a small prayer for strength and forgiveness.

Holding the gun behind her, she went into the living room, one wobbly step at a time. Kiel's back was to her and she moved near, feeling her eyes burn and the trickle of tears on her face. It was Mac forcing her ahead now; she knew that, but it was what she had wanted. Chips watched her, his eyes big, aware that something was about to happen.

Then Kiel was on his feet, swinging to face her. She clutched the gun tight; but the wariness in his eyes forced her hand and she brought the gun into sight, leveling it at him. He paused in indecision and she knew she should shoot. She saw his glance dart to Chips and she wondered why he didn't do something.

Kiel edged back. His face was hard, devoid of its first surprise. Her finger tightened on the trigger.

The shot blasted out and bounced from the high ceiling. Chips ran behind a chair as Kiel crouched, then straightened, unhurt. There was a clean hole in the overstuffed chair where the bullet had buried itself.

Kiel moved fast toward the hall and Carol followed; but with each step, her hand locked tighter around the gun and her finger refused to move on the trigger. Still she went after him, out into the shadows; and as the darkness touched her shoulders, a great fist pounded at her mind and she cried out, reeling forward, the gun falling from her hand.

Kiel grabbed her and shook her roughly. His breath was coming harsh and shallow. He had been afraid.

"You tried to kill me!"

"No!" she clutched at him. "I shot the gun; but I knew I couldn't hit you, Peter. I couldn't hurt you."

He held her off with strong arms. "I thought this was done with," he growled. "I thought we understood each other and accepted each other. I didn't want to touch you again; you know that. Why did you force me to do this?"

"They said I had to," her voice went on alone, and she knew she wasn't in control of herself. "Ray and Will said I had to do it — for humanity."

"And you let them use you?" His voice was full of disgust.

"They said that you're using me. That's all, just using me."

"And how do you feel? Would you care, even if it were true?" He stared hard at her. "Would you?"

"No," she answered blankly. "I — I love you. I love you."

There was no satisfaction on his face and he thrust her from him, picking up the gun. "It's no good," he said. "I don't want to hear it. Not when I'm putting the words in your mouth."

He shook the bullets from the gun and put them into his pocket. Carol felt herself relaxing, the fist releasing her. Kiel's touch was gone, and she was alone inside her body. She went back into the light, staggering against a chair.

Then Kiel was turning her to face him again, the anger diminished. He asked: "What do you intend to do now? Are you going to try it again as soon as you have me sufficiently at ease?"

"No," she stated frankly. "I can't kill you."

"You said that before. Why?"

"I don't love you, if that's what you're thinking. I didn't want to hurt you for the same reason I wouldn't want to hurt anything. I'll just leave you and be done with it."

"No!" He hardened. "You are not going to leave me."

Carol jerked out of his grasp. "Of course you can force me. I can't do anything against your will. But what good would that do? You said you didn't want a puppet."

"And I don't. But you'll stay anyway. I'll put it very bluntly, Carol. Either you stay with me, and be decent about it, act as a wife — wholly — or your friends will pay the penalty."

CHAPTER EIGHTEEN

Ray didn't want to hear any explanation; Carol had failed them, that was all. Will was angry at the rest for suggesting that Carol attempt the thing in the first place. Somewhere along the way he had split from the others, going a parallel course but a different one.

Kiel's next phone call came as a shock. He asked them to come to his home, not for the pleasantries of dinner but for a definite purpose. He didn't want Neilson; only Ray, Will and Mac.

Mac was astonished and said to Kiel, "How much do you expect us to believe? After Carol and all —"

"Are you still dwelling on that?" Kiel said, chuckling. "I've forgotten it. I have an offer to make — a proposition. Are you interested or not?"

*****

The night was bright with the great form of Orion dominating the sky, and the clear air held a crispness that drew the coats of the three men about them and squeaked snow under their feet. Carol was long in answering the ring. Her eyes misted over as she asked Ray if he would take the car home with him before it was too late. Ray agreed, promising to fatten him up for his return.

Kiel welcomed them with his usual aplomb and arrogant sureness of his place above them. But he didn't offer drinks or geniality. He couldn't, in the light of the expectancy radiating from them.

He began with flattery: "I admire your good sense in coming here at all. Most men, I'm afraid, would refuse."

"You said you had an offer to make," Ray said, eager to get on with the real business of the invitation.

"I have." Kiel smiled. "And the only way to make it is bluntly. You've come a long way. I've watched you do it, but now I think you're through. It's a stalemate. Therefore, it's time you followed your own adage — if you can't beat them, join them."

Three shocked faces riveted on him, but he met them squarely. "I admire your courage and resourcefulness. You've proved yourselves *and now I want you with me!* It's as simple as that. It should answer many of your questions: why I've left you alone and let you run your course of anger."

Ray's angular face grew tense. "Are you saying that you've decided to 'take' us now? That you want us under control?"

"No," Kiel assured. "It can't be that way. It must be free will on your part. I said I liked your courage, your resourcefulness. Those things would disappear if I took control of you."

They didn't move, offering neither a yes nor a no.

"There will be great compensations," Kiel hurried on, exasperated by their silence. "I'm offering you the world, don't you understand? I'm offering you wealth and power, in exchange for your cooperation. I've had you spotted from the beginning just for this purpose. Why else do you think I even let you find me? Or talked so openly to you? I wanted you to understand. You passed all my tests and now I want you to work with me. The next steps will be harder ones, and I'd like confederates."

Will had been waiting through the long speech, more inflamed with every word. "What do you think we are, Kiel? Power, money — in exchange for —"

"Sit down," Kiel commanded, black eyes flashing hard. Will took one angry step forward, then surrendered.

"No, he's right, Kiel," Mac said in Will's defense. "You didn't actually expect us to agree to this, did you?"

Kiel sighed, impatient.

"Yes, I expected you to agree. If you don't agree, you stand to lose everything. If you help me, I promise you, you'll always be safe — be yourselves. Think about that. Do you want to throw your lives away for misplaced loyalty to a bunch of weaklings who were born to be ruled in the first place? You should be grateful to me for offering you this chance."

Ray snapped: "You wouldn't be offering if there weren't something in it for you."

"I admit it — I can use you, but you're not vital. If you don't agree, my plans will be delayed; but the only difference in the final outcome will be three extra men to walk stiff-legged around a chair, where there could have been three thinking men."

Will leaped to his feet. With one jump, he was upon Kiel, hands clenched about his throat, pushing him backward. Kiel countered physically, trying to break the hold; but it wouldn't be broken. Kiel was panicked, his face convulsed with redness.

Then, in one instant, it calmed; and a terrible force permeated the room. Will screamed, agonized, let go his hold, and toppled sideways, falling like a tall building cut off at the base.

Ray and Mac were stunned to inaction, for Will's blood was spreading a red circle about the carpet, pouring from a great crack in his skull.

Kiel clutched at his throat, hobbling away from the body, his balance gone. He coughed twice, then turned, wary — ready.

"Stupid, emotional animal," Kiel hissed.

The words brought Ray to life, flooding his cramped muscles with anger. He strode forward, then halted as Kiel focused on him.

"Monster!" he accused. "Monster!"

"Because I defended myself?" Kiel's eyes almost hurt as they met and caught Ray's. "I understand why he did this. I *know* him, don't forget that. It wasn't for humanity — it wasn't an act of courage. It was personal. Entirely personal. He paid for it!"

Kiel's voice was malicious. "And now *you* have a problem. What will you do with the body?" As Ray advanced again, Kiel warned: "Do you want to double the problem? Take your friend and get out. This thing has gone far enough. It's over! I don't want to see you here again — either of you."

"Now you're afraid, is that it?" Ray spat. "Now your offer doesn't hold?"

"That's laughable. I made a promise — a promise I have already broken in part. I intend to keep the rest. It was foolishness to even think I could deal with blind animals. Pick up your friend and get out."

Ray stood undecided a moment more, then went to Will and wrapped an afghan tight about the body and covered the broken skull.

"I'll bring Chips," Carol cried, running for the stairs.

Ray didn't wonder how Carol could be so worried over the cat when one of her best friends lay dead at her feet. He knew the answer because he felt the pressure in his own mind.

CHAPTER NINETEEN

Chips reclaimed the house like a king returning from exile. Ray felt a close kinship with the life that stirred beneath the striped fur. Chips, too, had fought a battle. He was weaker than Ray, but not in courage.

For three days, Ray fought with himself, forcing the sight of Will away. To ease his depression, Ray rummaged through some of Professor Grayson's papers. He hoped he might find some answer in them.

He found a list of names and addresses. One of them was simply 'Jenny,' with a question mark. The address belonged to Jenny Peck. It was a list of Grayson's telepaths. Eight of them were in the city, where they had moved to be near someone who understood them.

Ray clutched the paper. These people could read thoughts. That meant they had some control over what Kiel called brain patterns. Control over their own, and maybe over others. It was enough if they could control their own. If they could set the pattern and focus it, all together, they might batter down the wall around Peter Kiel!

Ray handed the list to Mac, quickly explaining what he had just realized. Kiel had thought Jenny enough of a threat to be frightened when her mind touched his and to kill her afterward. Ten Jenny Pecks could unite their patterns and force him down.

"But how?" Mac protested. "They don't have Kiel's special power. They can't kill with their minds."

"We don't know that. They've never tried it. Anyway, it's just a matter of being stronger than Kiel to control him. That's what he said — the strong minds win, the weak minds lose. He said Chips bothered him with his hate patterns. If our eight telepaths concentrated on sending hate, what might that do to him?"

Mac sucked at his pipe. "You may be right. It's more to my liking than anything else, so far; but do you think these people would risk it?"

"I can't answer those questions until I've talked with them," Ray said. "But they're good people, and they worshipped Professor Grayson. When they know who killed him, they'll want to help."

*****

The telepaths listened with an interest which quickly changed to horror and then to anger. What they saw in Ray's mind was convincing, and they agreed to join him without question.

He made arrangements with them — five men and three women — to get in touch as soon as a workable plan was plotted. Neilson had come up with one thought. They must discover if Kiel was the only one of his kind who knew about Earth.

Carol was the only hope there, for Kiel had forbidden them his house. When Ray asked her to come over, he found her willing. Will's death had shaken her beyond loyalty.

While they waited for her, Ray brought out a map of the city, looking for the right spot to place the telepaths. It had to be near Kiel. Their power couldn't extend too far and remain potent, while his could obviously extend as far as he chose to send it. One of the telepaths lived only four blocks from the big river house, and his home was chosen as the battleground.

The generalship of the battle had to be given into the hands of a telepath, the man who owned the house they would use. They invited him over. His name was John Marker.

He arrived at Ray's house before Carol; and the men put their heads together, outlining the plan. As Mac had predicted, Marker didn't see anything strange in the idea of a mental battle.

"The idea," he said, "will have to be death. I don't know if we can kill his man, but I have an idea that we can."

"How so?" Mac asked.

"Because he's attuned to mental gymnastics. They make up his whole life. Therefore, he should be susceptible."

The doorbell's ring shot Mac to his feet, finger to his mouth in a shushing gesture. "That will be Kiel's wife," he told Marker. "Don't say anything in front of her. He'll pull it out of her the moment she gets home."

Carol's face was haunted as she met Ray. "I came as soon as I could," she murmured. "I had to wait for Peter to go out." She slipped her arms out of her fur coat and let it fall into Ray's hands. Suddenly she caught his arm, her eyes desperate. "Ray, I'm so sorry about Will. You can't know —" She waited for an incriminating remark, but none came. "I have to tell you, no matter what happens. I can't let you go on thinking that I'm rotten — that I'm actually in love with him. I *have* to stay there, Ray — for you. The promise Peter told you about — he promised me that as long as I stayed with him, as his wife, he'd leave you alone. Will was included in that, but it didn't work out for him. Peter has some strong code of honor that I can't understand. To him, a promise *must* be kept. It has something to do with the way they live that makes a promise their only security, and it's so ingrained in him that he can't go against it even now. What happened to Will shook him badly. So I know you're safe no matter what you do so long as I stay with him. I want to help, but that was another part of the bargain. I'm not to attempt to go against him again. Do you understand?"

Ray reddened, ashamed of the things he had been thinking.

A happy "purrrtt" announced the bouncing arrival of Chips, tail high in greeting. Carol scooped him into her arms. "Tiger," she purred back at him, "you're fatter already, bless your furry heart." The cat plastered her face with sharp-tongued kisses, squirming joyously. "It seems so good to have him this way again," she told Ray. "I was afraid that it was too late — that Peter had taken some vital part of him that wouldn't return."

"Not that cat," Ray laughed. "He's been tearing the house apart. Bring him with you. Mac has some questions."

In the living room, when Carol's face lit in recognition, Ray had a bad moment. He'd forgotten that Carol would already know John Marker.

Mac came right to the point. "Carol, has Kiel ever talked to you about how he came here?"

"Yes, quite often. He was a scout. Something went wrong with his ship and it crashed."

"Yes, but were there more of his kind nearby?"

Carol's forehead wrinkled in thought. "The way I remember it, a big ship, carrying these scouts, anchors in space and lets them out to explore. Each has a huge assigned area. When something happens to a scout, they cross his territory off and forget about it. He says they value life; and if one man doesn't return, they don't want to risk losing others. Every death means a vast reshuffling of controlled minds at home."

They were silent, thinking separate thoughts. Only the sound of Chips's purr vibrated in the room. Then, Mac surprised them all by asking: "Do you have an extra key to the house?"

Carol hesitated only a moment, then opened her purse. "You can have this one," she said. "But don't tell me why you want it."

"I wasn't going to," Mac answered.

*****

At four, a car stopped in the street; and when Ray glanced through the window, he jumped up, nervous. The car was Kiel's creamy convertible, and the tall man was heading for the door.

Carol rushed to put on her coat. She said quickly, "One more thing — Peter plans a trip to Washington in two weeks. So anything you have in mind, do it soon."

The doorbell cut her off. Kiel stared at Ray calmly, then looked past him to his wife. "Carol?"

"I'm sorry," she said. "I didn't notice the time. I'm ready."

"Come along then."

"Thanks for the coffee — and for Chips," she called as she went out. Kiel limped behind her. He looked somber in the blue, black-belted overcoat; and his lack of conversation made his halting figure menacing.

"That was close," Mac sighed. He'd had a tight hold on Chips all the time Kiel was there.

"So, that's Kiel," Marker commented. "He isn't so frightening."

"You didn't attempt —" Ray didn't finish, holding his breath, afraid the plan had been given away.

"No, I kept to myself," Marker replied. "But for the split second he looked at me, I felt it. I didn't know there could be a physical sensation to telepathy."

"He's not a telepath," Ray stated. "It's something entirely different. Can you handle him?"

"We'll try, that's all I can promise." Marker's face was set, grimly determined. He spread the map of the city over the coffee table; but the map was soon blotted out by the striped body of Chips, who decided the crinkly paper was a fine place to sprawl and capture the attention of the men around it.

CHAPTER TWENTY

One week later, on a night when new snow covered the ground and fell in blowing sheets before the wind, John Marker's house opened its door to eleven people in succession. The number was filled when Ray shook the snow from his coat and came into the light. Everyone looked at him, but no one said a word.

Ray said only what he had to say to complete the plan. "I made the call. They're spending the evening at home."

Silence closed back and the ticking of the mantel clock became unduly loud. Marker carried it out. When his footsteps died away, there was nothing left but breathing and the small noises a group of people make when they swallow. They were in a vacuum all their own, and the rest of the world was gone.

Marker took the center of the floor. "We have three minutes to prepare," he said quietly. "You may take your positions now." The seven people lifted their chairs to face the wall. Marker addressed his next command to Ray and his two companions. Please keep absolute quiet. We need complete concentration. Are you ready?"

The three nodded. Marker spoke to the backs of the people before him. "We will begin to work. Keep your thoughts on this room, joined together, until I give the signal. Then, throw them outside with the one emotion and the one thought. I'll direct you in; and at the first sign of reaching his mind, throw yourselves at him full force. We must take him by surprise." Marker took his chair. "Begin now," he ordered. "Call out your names."

Ray waited for the names, but nothing came. There was a bare perceptible change in the shoulders before him — a tightening, a lifting — and he knew without being told that John Marker had given the signal and was now leading the combined minds outward over the four blocks to the white house by the river.

Peter Kiel sat in his customary chair, reading the evening paper. Suddenly, he was on his feet, eyes wild, clutching at the back of the chair. He slapped his hands to his temples, took two halting steps, and fell to his knees, a cry pushing from deep inside him. Carol ran to him, calling his name. She knelt down and grabbed his arms. His hands caught her in a frenzied clench, and his head arched against her shoulder.

Another soft whimper came from him; and he let her go, his face grotesque in frozen concentration. He pulled himself up to lean on a chair, his eyes staring at the wall. A deep breath that turned to a sigh echoed in the room, and he stood a bit straighter.

Carol clutched at him but he was unfeeling, fists clenched on the upholstery, his teeth biting into his lower lip until it bled in a red line down the side of his chin. He smashed his fists down once, as though destroying something beneath them, and hobbled into the hall, seeming to need physical action to escape the pain that was tight on his face. He used furniture for support until he reached the newel post, then pulled himself upstairs by the railing.

*****

Nothing broke the silence in the room around Ray. The backs were tense; but the people were quiet, and thirty seconds had ticked by on his watch. The tension was a force in itself.

It shattered instantly in a scream which started from the throat of one of the women, broken off in full voice. She stiffened, toppled backward in her chair, and rolled out of it, blood seeping from a tiny crack in her skull.

A man turned around, horror bent on his face; but the others remained at the wall, bending farther forward, hands clenched in their laps. The lone man rushed out of the room, retching; and Neilson trailed to help.

The place turned into a hell as another deep groan vibrated out and a man reeled from his chair, ran three steps and stumbled to the floor. A third babbled incoherently and staggered away from the group. Mac grabbed him, covering his mouth to stifle the screams; but they came out anyway, garbled and wild.

"Stop it!" Ray shouted. "Stop it! Marker!"

He had to reach the man but was afraid to touch him. But compelled to take the chance, he caught Marker's shoulders and shook him until sane eyes swiveled to meet his. One look at the floor, and Marker went down the remaining line of three people, shaking and slapping until they were back in the room mentally as well as physically.

Everything was still but the babbling of the man in Mac's grip. Then he stopped, too, leaning against Mac, limp. Mac lowered him to the floor, felt for a heart beat, and shook his head.

"Dead," he said. "It's just as well. He was insane."

"We can't just stand here and let him pick us off one at a time!" a woman shrilled. "I can still feel him."

Marker hurried her to the kitchen, talking fast. The rest of them stared at each other, afraid, waiting to see who would be the next to fall.

Marker dashed back, shouting, "Go home! Scatter! Give him time to calm down and maybe he'll leave us alone."

The telepaths grabbed coats and mufflers. Two of them forgot their cars and ran down the sidewalk, leaving deep tracks in the snow. The back door slammed and the woman from the kitchen fled by the window without a coat, then flooded her car, stamping on the starter again and again.

Ray tried to take the situation in hand, covering the three bodies with blankets while Mac mixed Marker a drink.

"I don't know what happened," Marker said at last. "For the first little while, we were winning. I heard him cry out and I know he fell. It was a surprise. When he started to fight back, we strengthened ourselves — but then — I don't know what happened. He suddenly grew and grew! One hundred times as big! As if he was pulling in energy from outside and throwing it at us. We weakened and started to break apart. He would have had all of us if you hadn't stopped it. I couldn't break away by myself."

"Of course!" Ray slammed one fist into his palm, damning himself. "He *did* draw energy from outside. He said he could do that. They weren't fighting one man — they were fighting the power of all of his minds. We overlooked that — the most important fact. What can I say, John? I'm sorry down to my soul —" Ray wheeled away, his breath catching in his throat. "I'm through! We can't fight Peter Kiel. He's too much for any of us."

Marker swallowed the rest of his drink and wiped his eyes. "What do we do now? He's a monster! A monster! What do we do with the bodies?"

Ray let anger build inside him and take over. "Help me, Mac." He went to the blanket-covered forms, rolling them tight and folding them at the ends. He lifted the woman's body and disappeared out the door.

Mac stood dumbfounded. When Ray appeared, he gasped: "What are you doing?"

"The only thing there is to be done. I'm taking these three people to Peter Kiel. He killed them, Mac; and he's going to take care of them."

The four blocks whizzed by under fast wheels. Ray braked opposite the garden door and ordered them out with the corpses, laying them in a row on the threshold. He pounded on the wood paneling until a shadowy figure moved behind the curtains.

Carol pushed the door open and peered into the darkness.

"A present for your husband," Ray growled.

Carol gasped at the three shapes at her feet and stepped back. Ray thrust the doors wide, legs apart, braced.

Kiel limped forward, his hair disheveled and a handkerchief nursing a cut on his lower lip. His eyes shot sparks at the men silhouetted against the snow.

"What is the meaning of this?" His voice menacing.

"We brought you the remains of the battle, Kiel. Three dead. You'll have to have the decency to explain them. We have no excuse for what happened tonight, but you don't need one, do you?" The pressure of Mac's hand on Ray's arm halted the flow of words.

Kiel said nothing, his silence more threatening than a harangue. Carol caught his arm. "Peter?" She tried to catch his attention. "Peter! Please!"

"Come into the house," Kiel commanded them. "Leave them there and get in here."

Kiel slammed the doors behind the. When he turned, the blood-soaked handkerchief in his hand, his voice held the sharpness they had been expecting.

"What did you expect to gain by this little melodrama? Did you think it might impress me? Let me warn you right now, I'm in no mood to be impressed. The whole thing has ceased to be amusing."

"One look at you and anyone could see that," Ray spat.

"And you're angry," Kiel snapped back, "because you know this whole thing was your fault. I told you that you had no chance, but you went on in your stupid way, and you've managed to bring about the deaths of five people. Now you're here, playing the part of a suffering hero to try and ease your conscience. I didn't like what happened tonight, Dr. Harper" — Kiel's hand shot out, pointed at Ray like a weapon — "and you're responsible for it."

"Peter," Carol cried, pushing his hand down. "You promised me!" She threw herself between the two men, her hands on Kiel's shoulders, trying to act as a barrier to the black eyes that bore over her head. "You promised!"

"You'll have to forget that promise, Carol. You saw what happened to me. I can't let it go."

"Do you want me to break my promise, too?"

Kiel retreated a few steps in quick decision. "You can thank Carol for your life, Dr. Harper," he said, without a trace of surrender. "Though, I don't think any action from me is necessary. I think you've been repaid enough by seeing your friends drop one by one around you and yourself never scratched. That should be enough to haunt a man. You're a very sorry picture. So eaten up with hatred — *for yourself* — that you're paralyzed."

Ray shrugged out of the grasp of his friends, belligerency melting from his body. His face wore a thick mask of defeat. "All right, Kiel, you've won. You're right about me. I think the best thing you could do for me right now is take me over, body and soul — turn me into a robot so I won't have to think any more. I'm giving myself to you, Kiel!"

There wasn't a smile on Kiel's lips, but there wasn't suspicion either.

"Get out," Kiel said softly, dabbing blood from his lip again. "Leave the bodies and I'll dispose of them. I'll give you your chance at funerals and the fuss you take with your dead. Just stay away from me — you turn my stomach."

Ray muttered one more beaten question, "When it is going to be, Kiel?"

"Soon. Very soon. But you needn't worry. You won't know when it happens."

CHAPTER TWENTY-ONE

There wasn't an ounce of fight left in Ray.

Six days passed in idleness until Mac reached the end of his patience and burst forth in a fit of anger. "This is ridiculous!" he snorted. "That one man can stand up against all of us — a whole country, when you get right down to it — is just plain ridiculous! He has us all cowed. So, what if people have to die? This is a war! I say, rout him out with numbers. He couldn't stop a mass advance of ordinary, determined people."

"He could, that's just the point," Neilson countered. "He could reach out and grasp control of them, turning them back to slaughter each other. He feeds on numbers. Given an opportunity like that, he'd grow even faster."

"Bah! The answer is no before it's considered."

"Maybe if we'd done more considering," Ray argued, "three people would have been alive today."

"Quit wallowing in false pity," Mac accused. "They don't care that they're dead. I'm sick of this conscience-searching. You know, Ray, I don't think you would kill Peter Kiel if you had him helpless in your hands right now."

"So?" Ray showed anger that Mac noted with an inward smile. "What's the difference? Carol said they were leaving for Washington today, and Washington means the end. What's left?"

"I don't know, but I'm going to quit this nursemaiding and find out. I had something in mind once."

Mac stamped upstairs and returned with a notebook, its pages scribbled with words he'd put down after his first interview with Kiel. He said Kiel's egotism would serve as a self-trap. He wanted to make good that prediction and goad Ray into helping him.

He set up a card table and worked intently, ignoring Ray's frequent glances, grunting every now and then as though something made sense. But soon Chips was in the middle of the table, reaching out to catch his pencil and dotting it with tooth marks.

"You're a nuisance, that's what you are," Mac scolded. "I'm trying to do something important, and you want to eat the pencil." Chips squinted his golden eyes and stuck his tongue out the briefest way. Mac reached across and ruffled the cat's head. "You've got more guts than the lot of us, boy."

Ray straightened in a sudden fury of concentration. Then he came to Mac belligerently. "Give me some of those papers, you old charlatan. I just had an idea."

Ray shuffled through the papers; but Chips turned to swish his furry tail across the writing, making him read in spurts and bobs. "I read someplace that cats can drive lions insane, and now I see why." Mac caught the tail and held it firmly.

Suddenly Chips's whole body was raised into the air and clutched close against Ray's chest in a squeeze of joy. Ray paraded about the room with the cat until Neilson flagged him down. "What's the matter with you?" Neilson grinned in spite of himself.

"This little pussycat just opened my eyes. The cat that can look at a queen — Puss in Boots; the cat that saved humanity from the rat can save humanity from the fox. Blessed be the cat and may his race increase."

"Explain yourself."

"Give me a chance to bring it out. It came all in a jumble." Ray placed Chips in the center of the table. "Do you remember what Kiel said that first night you had dinner with him, Mac? Just as we went out the door?"

"He said we should be grateful because he had given himself a handicap."

"And do you know what that handicap was?" Ray made a sweeping gesture. "Chips! *Chips was his handicap.*"

"How did you arrive at that?" Mac was confused.

"It's all in the notes, but I've been too stupid to see it. Kiel told us that he can't control cats. He said that cats act as a jamming device to him. We made our mistake in believing that Kiel meant the jamming only kept him from controlling cats. He meant just exactly what he said — that the cats jam *him*, period.

"Do you remember how Kiel always kept an eye on Chips when the conversation got violent? Well, I've got the reason. It's the same reason Carol clung to the cat all the time she was under Kiel's control. He couldn't get a really firm hold on her with Chips around because the cat's brain broadcast jammed his own pattern — took the bite out of it."

Ray cleared his throat, dry with excitement. "A lot of things fit now. The night Carol tried to kill Kiel, she was out of the room — away from Chips — when he caught her mind. That friend of the Babcocks'; why was he alive and able to give us a description of Kiel?"

"He had a cat!" Mac said slowly. "But the Masons had a cat, too."

"From what Will said, that was a barn cat. If they had let it in the house, they might be alive today."

"I don't see the point," Neilson grunted. "What good is a cat, even if he can do what you say?"

"No *a* cat. *Lots of cats!* If one cat can impair Kiel's power enough to act as a jammer, what could twenty cats do working together?"

"Yes!" Mac gloried in the idea. "What good would Kiel's extra minds do him if his power lanes were jammed? I've got the key to Kiel's house and we can give him a welcome-home party when he comes back from Washington."

Getting their hands on twenty cats was no problem. Chips made one; they cut the number to sixteen with the help of one of the telepaths, then went to local catteries and bought fifteen cats. They brought six of them home and the house turned into a howling mass of felines, a Siamese setting up the loudest protests. Chips retired upstairs, determined not to mingle with the invaders.

They learned the date Kiel would return by the simple process of calling his cook and asking her when she was to report. Everything had to be ready by ten-thirty Tuesday night; the cats; the men; and the little group of telepaths Neilson insisted on holding in reserve, ready to enter the house and finish up. He phoned Washington and ordered four men sent up — men not exposed to Kiel.

The anticipation of waiting was exhilarating after the depression. Tuesday morning dawned sunny, and they made their first trip to Kiel's house to check the setup.

The neighbors on both sides had gone to Florida to escape the nastiness of February, and that cleared the area for a length of three city blocks. They made a close check of the walls before entering the house. They didn't want to lose any cats. It was enough to ask them to go up against Kiel.

CHAPTER TWENTY-TWO

Peter Kiel paid the taxi driver, picked up the two suitcases, and walked with Carol to the door. She bent to unlock it and they stepped inside without switching on the lights. Moonlight flooded through the windows with a white, murky gleam of its own.

"It's good to be home again," Carol sighed, weary in spite of the cushioned plane seats. She looked back for Kiel; but he stayed by the door, the suitcases in his hands. "What's wrong?"

"I don't know," his voice was soft, his head cocked, listening. "I feel uneasy."

"I'll get the light," she said, moving toward the living room. "Come on in and relax."

His halting footsteps trailed behind her, and then a sudden noise stopped her short of the switch. It hissed out of the moon-patched darkness with a moist, windy sound. She ran the last few steps and filled the room with the yellow light of electricity.

A grey shadow disappeared around the opening. "It must be Chips," Carol answered, curious. "How do you suppose he got here?"

Kiel dropped the suitcases with a thump and went to investigate. The kitchen light revealed a fat, grey Persian cat staring at them with menace in his eyes.

"It's not Chips!" Carol cried, but Kiel wasn't by her side.

"Look," he called from the living room, an edge in his voice.

She found him facing two more cats who sat hunched, noses raised, as soft hissing sounds came from their mouths.

When Kiel turned, there was apprehension in his eyes; but even as he reached for Carol, she cried: "There's another one coming out of the dining room, Peter. What's going on? Where did — ?" Kiel jerked away, headed for the hall, unsteady on a suddenly weak leg. Carol grabbed him. "Wait. What are you doing?"

"Let me go!" He wrenched out of her grasp, ran to the front door, and twisted the knob. It didn't give. He jerked and tugged and rattled the latch, then slammed his hand on the wood. "Did you lock this?" he cried, desperation masking his face. "I've got to get out, don't you see?" He stumbled to the newel post and caught himself before he fell, his legs refusing to hold him. "They're coming, Carol! I feel them. Help me!"

She stood frozen, confusion clouding her brain. The sound of a car whirred in from outside and doors banged shut. Kiel started to pull himself up the stairs using the rail for support. Chips appeared at the top to stare down with yellow eyes, and another cat moved in place beside him, crouching.

"Get them out of here!" Kiel yelled. "Look at them!" Carol followed his pointing finger to the foot of the stairs where four cats had gathered. They crept upward, one step at a time, keeping careful distance, but stalking the man who made reflections in their eyes.

A noise at the door, the sound of a key being thrust into the lock, whirled Kiel about, fierce concentration on his face. "It's Ray," he said. "Ray Harper!" His black eyes fastened on the door, his forehead creased; but the key turned in spite of him.

"Carol!" he cried, stretching out his hand to her. "Help me — please! They'll tear me to pieces."

The knob moved and Carol moved with it, charging up the stairs to where she caught hold of Kiel and helped him the rest of the way. She hurried him into their bedroom, not understanding, but compelled by the panic in him. A growl met them from the satin-covered bed and a Siamese cat leaped down. With a sound like twenty babies crying, Chips and the others closed in, arching around the door.

Sharp shouts echoed from below, mingled with the growling hisses of the cats and the click of more cat feet on the hall floor.

"Why did I come up here?" Kiel hobbled to the window and peered outside. "They're going to kill me," he said flatly, voice dull. "They've found a way."

"No!" Carol cried, clutching his shoulders.

"Help me, then." He clutched her tight, his hands desperate. "You're all I have. *Don't let me die!*"

He was pleading, and Carol felt the futility of the trap. The cats crouched and the men ran on the floor below. The cats' bodies were billows of fluffed fur running in ridges down their backs, and their red tongues flashed as they hissed.

New voices were added to the shouting, banging through the house, then everything hushed to silence. Dead silence.

With a whimper that was more animal than human, Kiel whirled beside her, under the impact of some invisible force. He twisted away and hobbled to the door, scattering cats before him. Carol called; but he didn't hear, proceeding down the hall away from the stairs, grasping at the wall and window sills to hold himself erect. He went into the next room and Carol rushed the other way, dazed and hysterical, with the blind notion that she could hold the intruders off. She leaped the stairs two at a time, her feet knowing the way in the blur of panic.

She bumped headlong into a red-faced panting Ray who was all arms, clutching at her, his body strong to keep her back. She struggled and struck out with her hands, battling his stubborn face, and broke free. In the doorway she found four faces that bloomed out of a past — a past of gentleness, of her father and his experiments. They were not gentle now, but contorted with concentrated hate. She pushed at them, slapping and screaming. "Stop it! Stop it!" Then Ray caught her and shoved her into Neilson's grip.

"Kiel's upstairs," Mac yelled. "Come on."

Ray dashed after him and they ran down the deserted hall, led to the right door by the fat shapes of fur that ringed it. They leaped the cats and burst into the room.

Kiel loomed before them, hesitated, and darted sideways, half-running, half-hopping the short distance to a side door. Then he was through, slamming it shut. Ray and Mac pushed against it, but it was locked.

A new sensation caught them. Mac jumped backward. "He's in there away from the cats," he gasped to Ray. "He's alone. I think he's got hold of me. Ray!"

In a desperate chance, Ray raced into the hall, shouted: "Bring those telepaths closer," and dashed to the front entrance of Kiel's new fortress. The cats were already there.

Taking a good start, he hit the door full force with his shoulder, his ears full of Mac's screams and the clamorous growls by his feet.

Urgency sent Ray battering against the wood until his shoulder was bruised to the socket and his arm was numb.

Then with a rending of hinges, the door burst open and the cats cascaded forward in a furry wave. Ray face Kiel, braced, eye to eye, ready to kill; then Mac heaved in beside him, weak but free, as the cats took over.

They advanced together and Kiel's fists clenched, but he backed as they maneuvered him to a corner. He retreated slowly, foot by foot, his movements weakening with each step backward.

"That was close, Kiel," Mac said, "but the closest you'll ever get."

"Keep away from me!" Kiel shouted. "You — stupid — animals." His voice began to slow and thicken.

"Be careful," Ray cautioned. "Give Marker a chance to work on him."

"Get away," Kiel groaned. "Away!"

He bumped against the wall, his body stiff as fright grew in his jet eyes. One hand pressed his head to fend off the hate radiating out to catch him from the animals and the telepaths below. With a tremendous effort he jerked erect and his eyes focused, shooting out at Ray. But there was only a slight tremor up Ray's back and he knew that was the extent of the power left in Kiel.

The cats closed in with their silent barrage and Ray's mind felt the immense forces playing on the man before him. Kiel was a cornered animal. His eyes darted back and forth, raking the room, pushed aside by the hissing cats. He started one way, then the other, trapped in one spot, pounded by invisible hands led by John Marker. His face twisted in fear and snarling hurt.

Then something broke inside him. His eyes clouded over, he shuddered, and tried to run. He stumbled four weak steps and toppled, clutching at the wall.

Mac and Ray reached him and turned him roughly forward, stemming his weak struggles. Words streamed from his mouth — unintelligible gibberish. Mac drew a quick breath and Ray muttered: "It's not English. Let's get him out of here. Take his left arm, and don't get too far from the cats."

They lifted Kiel between them and forced him to walk, leading him along the hall. The cats followed silently. Kiel shook under Ray's hands, trembling until it seemed he would break apart, mumbling on and on in the strange tongue.

Mac was triumphant, his hands hard on Kiel's shoulder, taking no chance with the man's potential. He muttered along with Kiel, "Grayson and Mason, Babcock and Betts, Jenny — This is for all of them. And *Will* — for *Will!*"

They started down the stairs and the telepaths gathered at the bottom. Kiel grew limp as they neared and Ray struggled to hold him up.

"Get Carol out of here," Ray called to anyone who could hear.

"She fainted," Neilson answered, his voice bristling with hate. "Bring him down. Let's see the god-among-men now."

The plop of furry feet echoed from behind as Ray and Mac reached the floor and hurried Kiel past the telepaths. He was gasping and panting, his black eyes glazed over, unknowing. They brought him to stand before Neilson.

"I was right," Neilson's words came fast. "The telepaths did the trick. He doesn't even know his own name. Look at him. We've won.

Ray kept his eyes averted from the man he held. There was something indecent about seeing him this way.

"What do we do with him?" Mac asked. "Do you want him? For Washington?"

Neilson's face hardened in deep lines. "Kill him!"

Ray stopped still, trapped by the two words. He looked at Mac, then back at the government man. "I can't do it."

For a brief moment, his hands fell away from Kiel's trembling arm. His reaction repeated in Mac and Kiel broke free. He stumbled away from them, bumping into furniture, head bent and his arms before him like a blind man.

The four telepaths approached as a body. Kiel reached forward, then fell to his knees, hands clenched tight against his head. The cats crept close to ring him about with shining, tiger eyes.

Kiel swayed — back and forth and back again — the muscles in his arms straining as he pressed his temples. A deep sigh came from his chest, rending the quiet. He shouted one clear but foreign word and crumpled. He sprawled, still, on the carpet.

"He's dead," John Marker whispered, his voice a shadow in the stillness. "He's all gone."

Ray reached for Mac's arm, and Mac searched automatically for the comfort of his pipe.

"It was like a burst of light," Marker continued, incredulous. "He was there, and then his mind closed in — and it was like a burst of light. He just died."

"*Peter!*" Carol screamed from behind them. "*Peter!*" She shoved by and knelt beside Kiel, lifting his head to rest against her legs. Her body shook and when she raised her face to Ray's, there was panic and accusation there. Slowly, though, it changed, with the realization of what had happened, what had been accomplished. Ray lifted her gently and helped her to a chair.

The hall suddenly transformed itself from a place of death to a place of relief, blossoming into smiles and nervous laughter. The telepaths were surrounded by twenty purring cats. A short man picked one up, chuckling "Partner." He looked about the room, challenging. "This one is mine. If there's any chance of Kiel's kind finding us again, I'm going to be prepared."

His voice brought the rest of them to action and Neilson took charge, clearing the house methodically. The cats were collected in their carriers one by one, petted and dispatched to new homes. In minutes, the flurry was over and quiet returned.

"I'm calling for an ambulance now," Mac told Ray softly. "You'd better take Carol home."

Ray lifted Chips and gave him to Carol. He felt no elation. Only relief to have it done and a new peace of mind.

"Something's gone," Carol muttered. "The electricity — the presence. I feel lonely."

"It's over, Carol." Ray drew her into the circle of his arm. "The only way it could be over. You can learn to be yourself again."

She nodded and walked beside him, eyes clear. Behind him, Mac whistled, "Ezekiel saw the wheel, way up in the middle of the air —"

Ray let Carol go on to the car and stopped for one last look at the covered body lying on the floor. "The little wheel turned by faith," he muttered, "and the big wheel turned by the grace of God. And by the grace of God, it has stopped turning."

He hurried to catch up with Carol. Chips pushed his nose against her neck to protect it from big snowflakes that cascaded around them — a soft bundle of chilly, contented cat.

THE END

www.ingramcontent.com/pod-product-compliance
Lightning Source LLC
Chambersburg PA
CBHW020145180626
46810CB00004B/1742